ABOUT that NIGHT

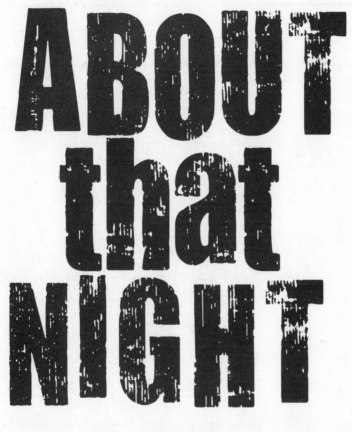

ABOUT that NIGHT

Norah McClintock

ORCA BOOK PUBLISHERS

Library and Archives Canada Cataloguing in Publication

McClintock, Norah, author
About that night / Norah McClintock.

Issued in print and electronic formats.
ISBN 978-1-4598-0594-1 (pbk.).--ISBN 978-1-4598-0595-8 (pdf).--
ISBN 978-1-4598-0596-5 (epub)

I. Title.
PS8575.C62A62 2014   jc813'.54   C2014-901559-3
                            C2014-901560-7

First published in the United States, 2014
Library of Congress Control Number: 2014935377

Summary: When Derek disappears in the snow, suspicion falls on Jordie.
What does she know about that night?

*Orca Book Publishers is dedicated to preserving the environment and has
printed this book on Forest Stewardship Council® certified paper.*

Orca Book Publishers gratefully acknowledges the support for its publishing
programs provided by the following agencies: the Government of Canada through
the Canada Book Fund and the Canada Council for the Arts, and the Province of British
Columbia through the BC Arts Council and the Book Publishing Tax Credit.

Design by Chantal Gabriell
Cover images by iStock and Shutterstock

ORCA BOOK PUBLISHERS
PO Box 5626, Stn. B
Victoria, BC Canada
V8R 6S4

ORCA BOOK PUBLISHERS
PO Box 468
Custer, WA USA
98240-0468

www.orcabook.com
Printed and bound in Canada.

17 16 15 14 • 4 3 2 1

To my girls

One

It's frigid—minus twenty—but Elise Diehl doesn't notice. Nor does she notice the way the wind catches the fronts of her housecoat, which she hasn't buttoned, and blows them out behind her like two quilted streamers. She is too enchanted to notice anything except the lacy flakes of snow that are floating down like so many tiny parachutists through the moonlit night. She sticks out her tongue. It isn't long before one lone flake lands there like a tiny, icy doily and melts. She spreads her arms and begins a long, languid whirl. She has always loved the snow. She especially likes it at this time of year, when multicolored lights twinkle on the massive Scotch pine in the middle of the lawn. The time of year when she and Mama and Daddy would bundle themselves into Daddy's big blue Pontiac and drive along the concession road,

NORAH McCLINTOCK

which is kept clear of drifts by the snow fences on either side, all the way to Grandma and Grandpa's house, where Daddy grew up and where Grandpa was born, right there in his ma's bed, and has lived all his life. The house, after they had stomped their feet on the porch and then stepped onto the oval rag rug inside, would smell of turkey and gravy and pie, and Grandma would help her off with her coat and boots and press a piece of shortbread into her hand. She loves Grandma's shortbread.

Elise starts down the driveway toward the glowing pine. She doesn't notice that the snow is accumulating faster now and that it won't be long before it is higher than the slippers on her feet. She dances down the driveway, beaming at the tree and its lights and wondering what will be waiting for her under the tree at Grandma's house. Grandma has beautiful colored-glass decorations that she inherited from her mother, who brought them all the way from England, wrapped in cotton and set into little compartments in the sturdy boxes where Grandma still keeps them. Grandma lights her tree the old-fashioned way, with little candles pressed into little metal candle holders with reflectors behind them to make them glow like fairy lanterns. Grandma strings popcorn and cranberries and garlands the tree with them. Later, after Epiphany, when the tree comes down, she takes off everything except these edible garlands, and Grandpa sets the tree out in one of the fields so that the birds can feast on the Christmas bounty. In a few places on the tree,

 2

Grandma hangs little wooden houses, painted in bright colors, with little doors in them that open. Elise hunts among the thickly needled branches for those houses. When she finds one, she is allowed to open its door and pluck out the piece of chocolate inside. Even if dinner hasn't been put on the table yet, she is allowed to eat it. It is the one time of year that Mama allows such an indulgence. Elise dreams about those little houses the whole of Christmas Eve. She dreams about them now as she reaches the end of the driveway.

She stands there a moment and looks across the street. What is that over there? Lights! The same bright multicolored lights that ornament the tree on her own lawn, but they seem to hang there in the air, a whole long line of them. And then she sees—there's a house over there. Its discovery stops her in her tracks. A house—where has it come from? She looks back at the house behind her, the one she lives in with Mama and Daddy. The house that Daddy so proudly built way up here, north of town, on a good-sized piece of land. He never intended to farm like Grandpa. But Daddy likes his space. He doesn't want to feel crowded by his neighbors the way the folks in town are—at least, that's how Daddy sees it. He keeps saying, "I don't know how those poor slobs can stand it, huddled down there cheek by jowl." Mama always looks shocked when he uses the word *slobs*. Elise always giggles. Daddy says it's not a bad word. He says that if Mama had been in the army like he was, if she'd spent the war years with all those other boys, boys who looked well brought up and well mannered, she would have been shocked. It seems that boys, left to their own devices, cuss like sailors. Or, as Grandpa puts it, like stevedores. Elise isn't sure what stevedores are. She thinks maybe they have something to do with bullfighting, like the picadors and the matadors in her favorite storybook, the one about the little bull who loves to smell the flowers.

Elise looks back at her house, and for a moment thinks she sees Daddy in the window. A snowflake falls into her eye. She blinks, and her eye waters. When she looks again, she can't tell if she imagined Daddy or if he has turned away from the window in disgust. Maybe he's calling Edgar Poole, who runs the RCMP detachment in town, the one that serves the whole county. Maybe he's asking him where in blue blazes that house came from. Elise would like to know the answer to that question. But even more, she would like to get to Grandma's house to help Grandma make shortbread. This is the year Grandma has promised to teach her and share her secret recipe. But first she has made Elise promise never to divulge the recipe to anyone, especially not to Mama. That's the one thing that injects a bit of sour lemon into every family occasion—the way Grandma feels about Mama. Grandma can't understand how her son, who fought against Hitler, turned around and married a German girl. Married her right over there in Germany, where he was stationed for nearly a year after the war. Imagine. Married an enemy!

Married one of those very same people who is responsible for her losing her elder son.

Grandma speaks to Mama. But she doesn't speak to her the same way she speaks to Elise. There is no warmth in her voice for Mama, and the smile on her lips, the rare times she offers it, is not the same smile that she flashes so easily at Elise or Daddy. Once, when Grandma didn't realize Elise was there, Elise heard her make fun of Mama's accent. Mama pretends not to notice when she is at Grandma's, but sometimes after she gets home, when she thinks Elise is asleep in her room, she cries, and Daddy comforts her and tells her that Grandma doesn't know her the way he does and that if she did, she would realize what an angel Mama is, why she's the best thing that ever happened to Daddy.

Who knows, Elise thinks, maybe this will be the year that Grandma sees Mama for the sweet person she really is. Maybe this is the year Mama will be the Christmas angel. Elise smiles at this thought and pictures Mama in a long white robe, perched on the top of the tree, the light from her halo making a big bright circle on the ceiling. She looks up the road, smiling to herself and thinking that this might also be the Christmas she tells Grandma how wonderful Mama is, perhaps when they are in the kitchen together, rolling out the shortbread and cutting it into star shapes and Christmas-tree shapes and bell shapes. Grandma loves Elise. Maybe she will listen to her. Maybe she will be nice to Mama this year—really nice, not phony-baloney nice.

As she stares at the thickening snow, Elise goes over in her head what she will say to Grandma. She thinks about the little houses on the tree. Grandma has been getting craftier about hiding them. Last year, there was one that Elise never did find. This year, she will not give up until she has located every single one, opened each of the little doors and popped each and every piece of chocolate into her mouth. What a nice thought.

She shivers and turns back toward the house. Her house. For a moment, she remembers who lives there now. A vague memory envelops her. House equals safety. House equals warmth.

TWO

Earlier that same night, Derek Maugham, seventeen going on eighteen, stares out the living room window of Jordie Cross's house. He has been staying with the Crosses for the past couple of days while his parents are out of town visiting his grandmother. This is the first time they have let him stay back instead of dragging him along, and that's only because he had to work up until two nights ago. At least, that's the reason his mother gave for finally waving the white flag. He knows, because his dad told him, that his dad thinks he's old enough to make his own decisions about whether he wants to tag along with them, especially when where they are going is to visit "some batty old dame," which is how his dad refers to his grandmother when Derek's mother is not around. Richard Maugham has never liked his mother-in-law, and now that she has remarried and is living with a man whom Richard calls a "goddamned miser," he likes her even less. Richard Maugham hates having to visit her, and he is grateful that his wife, who makes the trek several times a year, insists on his company only at Christmas. Richard goes because he loves his wife and because it's more trouble than it's worth to tell her no.

Derek has been insanely happy these past few days. He is madly in love with Jordie—how could he not be? She is smart and pretty and funny—and she likes him. That's the part he still can't believe. She likes him, and she doesn't seem to mind when he calls her his girlfriend. She's been his girlfriend for two months now, a status he dates from the first time he kissed her. He'd thought he was dreaming, fantasizing right there in the front seat of the car, or that maybe he'd drifted off while they sat parked there, but it turned out neither was true—it turned out it was real. She smiled at him afterward and told him how much she appreciated his difference.

"Difference?"

"You're reliable," she said.

"That's different?" If it was, well, vive la différence!

Being here in this house with her is like taking a stroll in heaven—no matter where he goes or what he's doing, there she is. She's sitting across the table from him, eating oatmeal at breakfast or a sandwich at lunch. She's making hot chocolate with marshmallows when he comes in from helping her dad shovel the driveway. She's beside him after supper at the sink, where he is rinsing dishes and she is putting them into the dishwasher. She's beside him on the couch down in the basement, where they are watching a movie or, if her little sister is miraculously absent, cuddling and kissing and touching each other. And when he lies in the foldout bed in the basement at night, he knows that she is two floors above him, in her pyjamas under her comforter, lying there and maybe, if he's lucky, thinking about him down in the basement. Life couldn't possibly be any better. At least, that's what he's been thinking up until now.

Now he is in the living room, checking up on her while her parents wait for him in the den, and Jordie is outside on the porch with Ronan Barthe. The guy showed up out of the blue—or so Jordie said when she answered the door and Ronan was standing there. Derek wants to believe her. But if this is such a surprise—a supposedly unpleasant surprise because, after all, Ronan is the ex-boyfriend—then why did he catch a look of excitement on Jordie's face, and why did she agree so quickly—she didn't offer any protest at all—when Ronan said he wanted to talk to her in private? And, more important, why has she been out there so long?

While he peers out the window at them, Jordie's kid sister Carly drifts past on her way to the den. Derek can't keep his eyes off them, Ronan in a leather jacket that can't possibly be keeping him warm in this subzero weather, and Jordie with a thick sweater wound tightly around her, held there by her arms, which are also wrapped around her. She must be freezing, but as far as he can see, she has made no move to hurry Ronan along so that she can get back inside where it's warm—and where Derek is waiting. Derek doesn't begin to understand what's so special about Ronan. He knows the girls all think he's cute, and grudgingly supposes he is, if you like those dark and dangerous looks and that sullen I-don't-give-a-fuck-about-anything expression. But Derek? Jeez, Derek can't stand the guy. He used to look at them together—Jordie and Ronan. They were a couple all last year, and Derek, who has been smitten with Jordie ever since he started high school, used to pray for the day she would come to her senses and dump Ronan's sorry ass.

Then it happened.

Status change: Jordie Cross declares herself single.

And Derek Maugham sees his chance.

Now, though, Derek remembers that he never managed to get to the bottom of what happened between Jordie and Ronan. She has steadfastly deflected all questions—"Why dwell in the past?"—and no one else seems to know or, frankly, even care, least of all Derek himself. Because, really, why should it matter to him if it doesn't seem to matter to Jordie? In all the time she has been with Derek, she has never mentioned Ronan, never spoken to him (that Derek is aware of), never even glanced at him across a classroom or in the cafeteria. She's been a hundred percent Ronan-free, which is exactly how Derek likes it.

But she is not Ronan-free now. He wishes he knew what they were talking about, but with the weather so cold, there are two tightly sealed doors between him and the front porch. But Derek watches them. He keeps his eyes on them the whole time, sees Ronan talking earnestly from behind the puffs of frosty breath, sees Jordie nod. What is she nodding about? What is she agreeing to? Why is she even talking to him?

It occurs to Derek for the first time that maybe the breakup didn't happen the way he's always assumed it did. Maybe Jordie didn't dump Ronan. Maybe it happened the other way around. And maybe Ronan has finally seen how wrong he was—only an idiot would dump a girl like Jordie—and has come to get her back. Maybe that's why she's nodding.

They finally stop talking, but instead of Jordie coming back inside right away, she stands there shivering—her whole body is trembling—and watches Ronan walk down off the porch, along the path that leads to the curb and then down the street. She doesn't come inside until he is out of sight. Then, instead of joining the family in the den, she says, "I need to get something," and she disappears up the stairs. She doesn't come down again for nearly an hour, during which Derek has to restrain himself from racing up to her room to ask her what the hell is going on, what Ronan wanted, why he came to the house. But Mr. and Mrs. Cross are both there in the den, watching *The Lion in Winter*. Mr. Cross has poured himself a Scotch, neat, and looks relaxed now that the Christmas festivities are over. Mrs. Cross is engrossed in the movie, which, according to Jordie, she has watched every Christmas that Jordie can remember (an odd choice, Derek thinks, until Jordie points out that the action takes place at Christmas). Even so, relaxed as they are, engrossed as they are, there's no way they will let him go up to Jordie's room, even if he's been up there plenty of times when they weren't around. All he can do is wait.

For what seems like forever.

When Jordie finally comes back downstairs, she hangs in the entrance to the den and speaks his name the way a teacher would: "Derek!" Like it's a command or a caution. Even her parents notice. For the first time since Ronan left the porch, Mrs. Cross's eyes stray from the TV.

"Is something wrong, dear?" she asks her daughter.

"I need to talk to Derek."

Derek excuses himself and gets up off the couch. He follows Jordie into the kitchen, puzzled by what he reads as ill humor, which only deepens when she closes the kitchen door behind them. She faces him, her arms crossed teacher-like over her chest.

"Did you take something out of my room?" It comes out like an accusation, as if she already knows the answer and the answer is yes.

"No. Why? What do you think I took?"

"Some jewelry."

Derek is stunned. "You think I stole jewelry from you? Why would I do that?"

"I know you have it, Derek."

"Have what?"

"My bracelet."

"What bracelet?" What's the matter with her? "Wait a minute. Does this have anything to do with Ronan?" He's never been able to say the guy's name without disdain, and Jordie picks up on it.

"What if it does?"

"What was he doing here anyway?"

"That's none of your business."

Is she kidding? Her ex-boyfriend shows up and the next thing he knows, she's accusing him of something— and it's none of his business?

"What was he doing here, Jordie?"

"Did you or did you not take jewelry from my room?"

"I did not. But, hey, thanks for the vote of confidence."

"Ronan says you did."

"Ronan says he saw me steal from you? Are you crazy?"

"He saw you with the bracelet."

Jeez, the bracelet thing again.

"He's wrong." Maybe even delusional—that wouldn't surprise Derek. "I didn't take anything from you. I would never do that. You know me better than that, Jordie." He peers at her. "Don't you?"

"He says he saw you with it."

"I know what he says. He gave me grief at school. Look, I didn't want to have to tell you this, but what he saw was the bracelet I bought you, and—"

"You bought me a bracelet?"

"I was planning to give it to you on New Year's Eve. That's our two-month anniversary."

Her face softens a little. "And Ronan thought the bracelet was the one he gave me?"

"Yeah. But it isn't. I bought it myself. The guy's crazy." Okay, maybe it's a mistake to say that. Her tiny smile of surprise and, just maybe, appreciation vanishes. Yup, definitely a mistake.

"He's not crazy."

"Okay, I'm sorry. But if you'd seen him…He was ready to take me on."

"Take you on?"

"Beat the crap out of me. I'm not kidding. You know how he is. But he was wrong. I don't have his bracelet. You want me to go home and get the one I bought and give it to you now? That'll prove I'm not lying."

She lets out a long sigh. He's not sure what that means, but then she says, "I'm sorry, Derek. I feel like I've ruined things for you. I must have misplaced that stupid bracelet." He likes the way she says it—as if Ronan has annoyed her with his petty problem. "I'll look again." She starts for the kitchen door. He catches her around the waist.

"Not now, okay? It can wait. Can't it?" He asks her if she wants to go back to the den and watch the movie with her parents or if she maybe wants to go down to the basement with him and watch a movie down there. In the end, she agrees to go downstairs, which would be perfect if Carly, fed up with Christmas tradition and having no patience for the slow pace of old movies, didn't decide to join them. Still, Jordie calms down and snuggles against him and stays snuggled until Carly, bored or tired or both, finally drifts upstairs. Derek is glad to see her go; he pulls Jordie closer and gets ready to kiss her.

But she wriggles away until there's a good chunk of sofa between them.

"Why would Ronan think you had his bracelet if you didn't?" she asks.

Jeez, that again! The way the question comes out, coupled with the frown on her face, makes him think she has been chewing this over the whole time they were supposedly watching the movie.

"You've seen the one he gave me. It's practically one of a kind. It's not one of those mass-produced things you can get in some low-end jewelry store."

"I never saw it."

"I wore it all the time, Derek."

"Maybe you did. But you weren't wearing it anymore when we started going out, and before that, it wasn't your wrist I was looking at. It was your eyes. And your face." That earns him a smile. "You know what it probably is? Maybe he's shortsighted, and he needs glasses. Or maybe"—he can't stop himself—"he's an idiot."

Jordie tenses up, which annoys Derek. If Ronan is truly her ex, she shouldn't care what Derek says about him.

But she does.

"Okay, I'm sorry I said that. Honestly, I don't know why he thinks I have his bracelet. I don't."

He reaches for her again.

She pulls back out of his reach—again.

"Did you take it because you were jealous of him?" she asks.

She's never going to let up.

"Okay. A, I didn't take it." There's a sharpness to his voice now that he doesn't try to hide. Everything was going along just great until that asshole Ronan showed up on the porch. "And B, what do you mean, am I jealous? What do I have to be jealous about? Ronan? You two split up, remember?"

She doesn't answer.

He doesn't know whether to press the point or not. They did split up. Everyone knows it. When it happened, everyone at school was talking about it, and they all pretty much said the same thing: it's about time. He certainly seconded that emotion. She's never talked about what exactly led to the breakup, and now he's wondering again what *did* happen. And, more important, who instigated it. Everyone assumes it was Jordie because, really, why would any guy, especially a guy like Ronan Barthe, who'd won the lottery when he landed her, be stupid enough to let her go? But the guy is strange. Everyone knows it.

"Jordie, are you telling me I should be jealous of Ronan?"

"Of course not," she says, but without the conviction he was hoping for. Without a smile. Without reaching for his hand, without sliding closer to him and snuggling up to him, without kissing him, not even on the cheek.

It's because of all of that, and because she still seriously thinks he might have stolen some stupid bracelet, supposedly bestowed by an ex-boyfriend—and because Ronan showed up the way he did, no doubt about it—that Derek decides to slip home and get the bracelet *he* bought for her, the kind of bracelet he knows she is going to love because it isn't some mass-produced thing either. It's special. He doesn't bother with a note. He plans to be back in a few hours, while everyone is still asleep.

Three

J ordie stays up late that night. In fact, she hardly sleeps at all. Long after Derek has slipped out of the house, she is sitting exhausted on her bed and surveying the wreck that is her bedroom. The contents of her dresser drawers are strewn across the floor. A half dozen or more purses have been upended and also lie on the floor. Her jewelry—almost all of it costume jewelry—is scattered across her dresser. The jewelry box is empty. Her closet door stands open from when she searched every pocket of every jacket and coat she owns.

Also searched: her desk drawers; both of her backpacks; the collection of vintage tea and cookie tins and boxes that she inherited from her grandmother, an avid collector, and which she has filled with makeup, more jewelry, trinkets and bric-a-brac, what she describes as "just stuff" when her mother asks how on earth she has managed to fill them all; the three mugs she keeps on her desk, filled with pens, pencils and markers; and the wicker ottoman that opens up and that she shoves all manner of things into whenever her mother nags her to tidy up. It looks as if her room has been ransacked by a thief searching for some specific treasure, or by a surly cop trying to pin a murder on her, or, perhaps, by a vicious little sister. But none of these is true. Jordie has done this damage herself.

It had started out so simple. Ronan showed up unannounced on her porch (she had forgotten how much she loved looking into those dark blue eyes of his) and asked for the bracelet back. Her first thought: tough luck, buddy, it was a gift, and it's mine now. She loves that bracelet. And if he wanted to get all pissy because their relationship hadn't worked out—his fault, not hers—then too bad for him. A gift is a gift: once you give it, it belongs to someone else, to do with as they please.

The thing though? He wasn't angry about it. If anything, he looked sad.

"I wouldn't ask if it wasn't important," he said to her out there on the porch. "You know that, right, Jordie? Did I ever ask you for anything, *ever*?"

No, he never had. But it's not the virtue he makes it out to be. The truth is, Ronan Barthe is a guy who can't bring himself to ask for anything from anyone, no matter what the circumstances. If he were drowning and someone were to appear on the shore, he wouldn't call for help. He has too much pride for that. It's either save yourself or admit your failure, because any man—this apparently applies only to men—who can't save himself doesn't deserve to live. It was part of the problem between him and Jordie. He never asked for anything. And because he never asked, he seemed to think she didn't have any right to ask either, not even for the things that don't require effort or expense to give, like maybe a phone call when he was going to be late or an explanation for why he was so clearly out of sorts, or just a word, one little word, to help her understand why he felt he had to put his fist through the wall in the chemistry lab, right in front of Mr. Thornbury.

"I need that bracelet, Jordie. I'll get you another one if you want. But I really need that one back."

She didn't ask why he needed it. If she knew him at all—and she wasn't entirely certain anyone could claim to truly know Ronan, but if anyone could, she guessed probably she was the one—he wouldn't explain anyway. So she said, "Sure." She said, "I have company right now, but I'll look for it later, and I'll get it back to you as soon as I can. Okay?"

He said okay, but even though she'd agreed to give him what he wanted, he didn't leave. Not right away. He stood there, frosted breath streaming out of his nostrils, as thick as cigarette smoke, and looked at her. Then turned and looked through the window into the living room.

"Maugham has it," he said.

"What?"

"Your boyfriend." Just the way he said it irked her. "He has the bracelet. Did you give it to him or what?"

"No." Why would she do that? "What makes you think he has it?"

"I saw him with it." He glanced at the living room window again, and this time Jordie followed his gaze. Derek was standing there, only half hidden by the curtain, peering out at them. "He's here tonight?"

"He's been here for a couple of days. His parents are out of town, and my mom said he could stay over." She knew what Ronan was thinking: *Your mom never said I could stay over. She never even liked to have me in the house.* What he said, though, was:

"Stay over? For how long?"

"Until his parents get back tomorrow afternoon."

Ronan digested this. "Yeah, well, he has my bracelet."

She let that ride—*my* bracelet, as if it still belonged to him.

"I'll look for it," she said. "I'll give it back to you."

Funny, it didn't occur to her to doubt Ronan when he said Derek had the bracelet. She isn't sure how she feels about that. On the one hand, as far as she knows and despite his many other faults, she is one hundred percent rock-solid certain that Ronan wasn't lying to her. On the other hand, what kind of person believes her ex-boyfriend's description of events when it flies in the face of the tale recounted by her current boyfriend?

The minute Ronan had left—after she'd watched him go, all the while wishing he would stay—she'd gone up to her room and checked the top drawer of her dresser, which is where she had put the bracelet after she and Ronan broke up.

It wasn't there.

So then, with Ronan's words still in her mind, she had gone downstairs and asked Derek if he'd taken it.

Accused him of stealing the bracelet from her room, in fact, and grilled him as if she were a cop and he were a thief.

He said he hadn't taken it, but did that put an end to it? Of course not. She'd let it eat at her for hours—for the whole length of a movie plus commercials—and then started in on him again. And he stuck to his guns: *I didn't take it, the guy's an idiot, and by the way, you ruined the (so-called) anniversary present I had planned for you.*

So she did what any sane person would do if her ex-boyfriend showed up and asked for a gift back (right?). She tore her room apart looking for the bracelet. But she didn't find it. What did that mean? Was Ronan right? Had Derek taken it? And if he had, if he'd stolen it out of her dresser, why? She could understand—she would never forgive it, but she could understand it—if he was jealous that she'd kept something Ronan had given her. She could imagine him taking it and throwing it away—because if she were with, say, Ronan, and he was hanging on to something from an ex-girlfriend, that was what she'd want to do (whether she would actually do it was an open question), right along with wanting to know why he was keeping something like that (which Ronan, being Ronan, would probably never tell her). But to steal it and then take it to school where Ronan could see it? That didn't make sense.

She swings herself off the bed. It's two in the morning. Everything can wait. But she knows she can't sleep, not with Ronan's face dancing in front of her eyes, not with these feelings in her belly, the ones she hasn't felt in months. Instead, she starts to put everything away. She works slowly, methodically, scarcely giving a thought to the bracelet. Instead, she's thinking about Ronan. He drives her crazy the way he never quite opens up, never talks about what he's feeling—well, except to kiss her and hold her, and she knows for a fact that he loves to smell her hair. Whenever he did, whenever he buried his face in it, he almost always smiled. He liked to hold her hand when they walked to and from school—and anywhere else, for that matter. He liked to go to the library with her, and when he was there, he actually did his homework, which wasn't something you could always say about Ronan.

By the time she has everything returned to its place and still hasn't found the bracelet, she is imagining how upset Ronan will be when she tells him it's missing. Derek must have taken it. Because if Ronan says he saw Derek with the bracelet, it must be true. She hopes Derek hasn't done something stupid, like get rid of it.

She's furious that he took it in the first place. Ronan would never do something like that, infuriating as he is in his own way. She'll get that bracelet back from Derek if it's the last thing she does. Then she'll give Derek a piece of her mind. In fact…she stops what she's doing. Oh, Jesus. She's going to break up with Derek. He isn't what she wanted after all.

Four

Police Lieutenant Michael Diehl, on leave for two months now, ever since his father-in-law died, jogs back up the hill, his heavy breathing sucking the frigid air deep into his lungs until they feel as frozen as his high-booted feet. The sky is thick with low-hanging gray clouds. It snowed all night, and it's going to start again soon. When it starts, it isn't going to stop for hours, maybe days.

Diehl's house—the one he moved into when he married Elise, the same house Elise grew up in and that was made over to her in her father's will—is just up ahead. But instead of turning in there, he veers right and runs—well, staggers—across to the foot of the Maughams' driveway. There's no trace of car tracks, but for all he knows they could have returned while he was out. He jogs up the snow-covered front walk and rings the doorbell.

No answer. He rings again. Still no answer. Okay, so they're obviously not back yet. Not that they would be much help. As he trudges back down the path to the driveway, he does what he should have done hours ago. He digs his cell phone out of his pocket and presses one of the pre-programmed numbers.

"It's Elise," he says to the voice at the other end. "She's gone. Again."

He listens to what the voice says, then goes inside. By the time a couple of patrol officers ring his bell, he's changed into dry clothes and has downed a cup of freshly brewed coffee. He knows the two officers—one on the job less than a year, bright, eager and ambitious; the other solid enough but never keen to climb the ladder, waiting for retirement and a pension that is less than five years away. He tells them how long he thinks Elise has been missing and where he's looked, and they diligently write it all down, asking a lot of questions, eager (especially the younger one) to make a good impression because, after all, he outranks them. In fact, he's their boss. He tells them everything he can think of—where he's found her before, where she likes to go on the days when she is able to express a preference, the places she used to frequent when she was a girl.

"She grew up right here in this house," he says. "And people like her, people with her illness, sometimes the only memories they can dredge up are memories from a long time ago."

"I heard that," the younger patrol officer says. "I read an article. It was about Holocaust survivors who develop Alzheimer's. They freak out, and I mean really freak out, because all they can remember is being back in the camps."

Diehl looks at the kid, impressed that he reads but at the same time sincerely hoping this isn't the kind of thing he'd say to a civilian whose loved one was missing.

Someone else rings the doorbell. Diehl goes to the door. It's Neil Tritt, and he's looking down.

"Looks like you need fresh weather stripping," he says.

Diehl can't begin to imagine what he is talking about.

"You're leaking heat," Tritt says. "The bottom of your door is frosted over."

If it had been any other day or under any other circumstances, Diehl might have laughed. Tritt is a born detective. He notices things that other people—other detectives—don't see. Like now. He looks up from the door and sees the expression on Diehl's face.

"Sorry," he mumbles. "Force of habit."

"Come in." Diehl bears no ill will. If anything, he's glad Tritt is here. He's grateful for someone he can really talk to. Tritt and Diehl came up at the same time. They patrolled together and made detective together. It doesn't seem to bother Tritt at all that Diehl is now his superior. They have the same easy, comradely relationship they've always had.

"Mike, how ya holding up?"

"It's cold out there."

"Was she wearing a coat?"

Diehl shakes his head. "I checked. All her coats are in the closet."

"Do you have any idea when she left?"

"Sometime between ten last night, when we went to bed, and eight this morning, when I woke up." His face twists in anguish. "I can't believe I didn't hear anything. Usually, all she has to do is move and I wake up."

Tritt lays a hand on his shoulder. "You look exhausted. You were probably worn out. I know I would be if I were in your shoes." He turns to the patrol officers. "I've got some more guys coming. I want everyone out there looking." Back to Diehl. "You got a recent picture?"

Diehl pulls out his wallet and extracts a head shot. "I had it taken last month at the mall. You know, just in case." His voice breaks. Jesus, another couple of seconds, he thinks, and I'll be sobbing like a baby. What will Tritt think? What will the patrol officers think? That this thing has broken him, that's what. He's off for two scant months and, what do you know, there he is, falling apart at the seams. Well, they can think what they want. You do what you have to do.

"Get copies made," Tritt says to one of the officers. "Make sure everyone has one. And make sure the lieutenant gets the original back. See that the local paper gets one and runs it. And the TV station. And remember—

in fact, tell everyone—she may not answer to her name. That's right, isn't it, Mike?"

Diehl nods. Sometimes she turns her head when he says her name. The rest of the time, it's as if she hasn't heard. Or as if he's talking to someone else altogether. Which he might as well be, because she sure isn't the same woman he married. Not even close. Not only that, but he can't remember the last time she looked at him with genuine recognition or said his name.

The two patrol officers leave. Diehl sinks down onto a chair. The temperature has dropped precipitously since last night. Since she wasn't wearing a coat, she'll be in trouble—unless, of course, she's managed to find shelter. And that's assuming she's had the good sense to think about something as practical as shelter.

Five

It's three o'clock in the afternoon, and still nothing. In another couple of hours, the sun will have sunk below the horizon, and then it will be up to the Christmas lights to cast what illumination they can. Three police cars sit on the road in front of the house. Tritt stands next to one of them, giving Diehl the lowdown. Diehl has been out most of the day himself, after his brief warm-up. Tritt is going over all the places they've looked—some of them are the same ones Diehl himself checked—and probing for other places Elise might be.

"Honestly, I don't know," Diehl says. "I feel like I don't know anything anymore. I thought I'd covered every place she's been. This town isn't that big."

A gray Chevy Impala crests the hill and slows as it approaches. Diehl and Tritt both watch it. It's Richard

Maugham's car. The driver's-side window whirs down as the car draws even with the end of Diehl's driveway.

"Everything okay, Mike?" Maugham asks.

"It's Elise. She's missing." He jogs over to the car.

"Missing?" Marsha Maugham, slim and still attractive at forty-eight, leans across her husband, her brow furrowed. "In this cold? I hope she hasn't been gone long."

"Since sometime last night or this morning," Diehl says. "I'm not sure. She got out of the house while I was asleep."

"Give me a minute to get changed and I'll help you look," Maugham says.

"We've been out since this morning," Diehl says. "Have a whole search party out." He glances at Tritt, who nods. "We'll be at it again first thing in the morning."

"We'll be there," Maugham says. "I'll get hold of Derek. He can help too."

"He's not home," Diehl says. "I rang your bell earlier to see if you were home yet—you know, to see if you'd seen her."

"He's been staying at his girlfriend's house," Marsha says. "He'd rather spend time with her than go to visit his grandmother."

"At his girlfriend's house, huh?" Diehl says. "Safe under her parents' watchful eyes, is that the idea? You sure he didn't sneak her over here last night?" He winks at Maugham.

"Well, we're assuming her parents have been riding herd on them," Maugham says. "But I guess you never know."

"Richard!" Marsha sounds scandalized by such a notion.

Maugham shoots her a look. "You're going to tell me your parents knew where we were all the time, never mind what we were doing?"

Marsha blushes. She glances at Diehl, clearly wishing he wasn't standing there.

Maugham is oblivious. "The minute I get hold of Derek, I'll ask him if he saw anything."

"That'd be great," Diehl says. "Thanks." He watches as Maugham steers the car into his driveway, the garage door sliding up to receive them and then down again, swallowing both car and passengers. Lights go on inside the house.

Diehl jogs back to Tritt.

Six

Jordie Cross listens to the first few words of the recorded message for the sixth time that day: "Hey, it's Derek. Leave a mess—" before pressing the Off button and tossing the phone onto her just-made bed. It's like a fever. Now that she's in the grips of it, now that she's made up her mind, it can't wait. She has to talk to Derek, the sooner the better. But this isn't the kind of thing she can say in a voice-mail message.

Well, she *could*. Lord knows it's been done before. But it's not the right way to handle it. It's the coward's way, the way of the dog, the loser, the asshole. And whatever else she is, Jordie Cross is *not* an asshole. At least, she hopes she isn't. There are enough of those in the world; there's no crying need for any more.

No, this isn't something you should do over the phone. This is something you have to do in person. Derek is not going to take it well, especially not after last night. He's going to be angry. He's going to accuse her of all kinds of things, probably starting by asking what the conversation with Ronan was *really* about and what he was *really* doing there. There's no way he's going to believe it was about what she told him it was about.

Maybe she should never have agreed to go out with Derek. He's *okay*. That's the best she can say, and she's surprised she's only just realized that now. Derek Maugham is okay. True, after Ronan he seemed more than okay. She'd been so grateful to be with a guy who actually talked. She's never had to guess what Derek is thinking or feeling. She's never had to walk on eggshells around him the way she sometimes did with Ronan. Derek is like a computer program—WYSIWYG. But okay isn't enough, obviously, because look what it's driving her to do. That's what's happening, isn't it? There isn't any other reason her heart is telling her Derek isn't the one, is there? She's not crazy, is she? Or, worse, she's not that cliché, is she? The good girl who is like a moth drawn to a flame, going for the wrong guy because he's more exciting or more challenging or, God forbid, because she thinks he will change for her? Maybe she is. Why else would she be in such a hurry to dump a guy who appreciates her and lets her know it in favour of a guy who is emotionally constipated?

Why?

Because the heart wants what the heart wants.

Because you can't build a relationship on one person appreciating, practically worshipping, the other person, not if it works just the one way, she as the object of adoration, he as the one on his knees. She wishes it was enough. She thought that it was, until last night. Now it's so obvious. Now she sees that she isn't giving what he's giving. There has to be some reciprocity. There just has to be.

Was there reciprocity with Ronan?

Be honest, Jordie. You know there wasn't.

Or was there?

That's the thing with Ronan. With silence. With not saying whatever it is you're thinking. You keep the other person off-balance. You make them wonder. Did Ronan love her? Does he love her now the way she's afraid she might love him? Or can you describe the whole thing in its simplest terms like this: Jordie is to Ronan as Derek is to Jordie? Because in truth, the one thing she wants more than anything else is to make Ronan happy. And this in spite of knowing, from experience, that making Ronan happy is like winning an Olympic gold medal. It takes gargantuan effort, more than can or ever should be demanded of one human being. But it's worth every second when you succeed.

What do you know, Jordie? I know that Derek isn't working for me. I know—I'm so sorry, Derek—I know I don't love him. I know that I feel selfish and guilty when he gives his heart to me the way he does and I can't give him mine. And I know that I miss Ronan. Seeing him up close like that, hearing his voice, catching the barest scent of him—I miss him. I want him back.

She pulls on her boots and coat. She winds her scarf around her neck and plunks a hat onto her head. She pulls on gloves. She sets out—and stops after a few blocks for coffee and to think, to work through in her head what she is going to say to Derek. One thing she is determined to do: be kind to him. He deserves that much.

She sets off again down the snow-covered sidewalk, turns right and heads north. But by the time she reaches the end of the block, her resolve wobbles. Not the resolve to do the deed, but the resolve to do it in person, the way, she tells herself, she would like it to be done to her. The right way. But is it? Is there a right way to break a person's heart if the end result is the same, if you leave the person in shambles? By email, by text, by phone, Jesus, by telegram, if that were still an option—is there really any difference? Will Derek be any less stunned by the news hearing it directly from her mouth while staring into her eyes than if she, say, texts it to him? Will he feel any better getting the personal touch? Even if he tells himself later that he should have seen it coming—and he probably will, he'll probably put it all down to Ronan's stopping by last night—there's no doubt that he'll be angry and devastated and bitter. Worse—is this what she's avoiding?—she won't be surprised if he cries. Derek tries to be a guy's guy. Occasionally, he tries to hide his feelings. But he's lousy at it. It's another of the things she found so alluring at first—his willingness to strip down to emotional nakedness in front of her.

But wait a minute. She's doing it again—putting things in the best possible light. She's possessed of enough self-awareness to know what that's all about. She's rationalizing: Derek has so many fine qualities; she can't deny it, so maybe she shouldn't do what she's planning to do. She's rationalizing *and* dissembling. It's not that he's willing to strip himself naked—the truth of the matter is, he's incapable of doing anything else. He couldn't hide his true feelings or hold in his tears if his life depended on it. And sure, a lot of girls might find that attractive, but she doesn't. Not anymore. Not now that she's seen Ronan again up close and felt the flutter in her heart that has been missing these past two months.

There, she's admitted it: guys who hide everything drive her crazy, but so, it turns out, do guys who hide nothing. Or, to put it the way another guy would put it, who can't keep their emotions in check. Who can't control themselves. It turns out, much to her astonishment, that she is not attracted to this type of guy after all.

By now the sky has grown overcast, a combination of gathering clouds and the steady, inexorable, late-winter-afternoon descent of the sun. If she doesn't hustle, she'll find herself stumbling home again in the dark, because there is no way Derek will offer her a ride after she says her piece. Or maybe he will. In fact, wouldn't that be just like him—*you've broken my heart, but the gentleman in me can't let you walk home alone in the dark and the cold.* He will insist that she accept a lift home. But there is no way she can allow herself to say yes, not if what she plans to say is going to stick. So better to get there fast, before the thought can even occur to him, while there is still some brightness, however cloud-muted, in the sky.

She picks up her pace. Within minutes she has reached the end of town and is cutting across the park to the hiking trail that runs most of the way up the hill. It's quicker than taking the road.

She makes it all the way up, up to the spot in the trail where a small path, buried today under the snow, leads to a flight of stairs, also buried, that leads up to the back of his house. This is the way Derek usually goes, although there is no trace of his passing today, not with all the snow they've had.

She circles around his house to the front door and rings the bell. His mother answers and smiles warmly at her as if she's welcoming a future daughter-in-law, which has always made Jordie squirm—as it does now, confirming for her that she is doing the right thing; if she wasn't, she would be grinning as idiotically as his mother is.

"Is Derek here?"

Mrs. Maugham's smile wavers. She peeks over Jordie's shoulder.

"Isn't he with you?"

It turns out Derek hasn't been home. Or if he has, he isn't there now. Jordie politely refuses an invitation to come inside and have a cup of tea while she waits for him. Instead, she goes back the way she came, pausing on her way down the hill to call home to see if Derek is there.

He isn't.

Seven

ive hours later, after Marsha Maugham calls Jordie
Cross, her son Derek's girlfriend, only to find that
Jordie *still* hasn't heard from him—"I would have called
you if I had, Mrs. Maugham. I *will* call you"—she feels
tears run down both cheeks and asks her husband if he
thinks they should call the police.

"And tell them what?" Richard Maugham says from
behind his newspaper. "That our seventeen-year-old
son, who is plenty old enough to stay home alone when
we leave town and who is probably screwing that girl
regularly—"

"Richard!" His wife is aghast.

"That our seventeen-year-old son is a couple of hours
late for supper?"

"He's not answering his phone."

"This is new?"

It is not new. In fact, Derek's use of call display as a parental-screening-out device is a constant source of frustration, irritation, anger and, occasionally, tears. The whole point of the cell phone, bought and paid for by Marsha herself, was that she wouldn't have to worry about where he was or what he was doing. But Derek seems to use that phone exclusively to make calls to nonfamily members—unless, of course, he runs short of cash or needs a lift somewhere.

"He'll be home when he's hungry," Richard says. "Unless that girl is a good cook."

"She says she'll call if she hears from him."

"Well, then," Richard says. "That takes care of that, don't you think?"

But it doesn't. Especially as the night wears on and the numbers on the clock flip to 12:00 midnight. Especially not after Marsha has left at least a dozen messages on her son's phone, five of them in the last hour. Especially when Jordie hasn't called yet and isn't responding to voice-mail messages either. And especially not when Richard is snoring beside her.

She takes the cordless phone from the cradle and carries it out into the upstairs hall. This isn't, strictly speaking, an emergency—at least, she's pretty sure the police wouldn't consider it one—so she has to call directory assistance to get the police nonemergency number. When an automated voice prompts her to press the number sign if she wants to be connected to a living, breathing body, she does so. Then ensues a ten-minute conversation with a police officer whose name she can't remember, and she is too intimidated to ask him to repeat it. The police officer tells her the same thing Richard has told her with increasing impatience: maybe he's with friends, maybe he's partying, maybe he's with a girl, he's almost eighteen, isn't he, do you have any reason to suspect foul play, does he have a medical condition you're concerned about? No? Well then, I suggest you wait it out, and if he doesn't turn up by morning, call his friends. If he still doesn't turn up, get back to us, and we'll take a missing-person report.

Marsha is in tears when she finally hangs up. Missing person? Her son? That can't be. It can't. Then she wonders how many other mothers have thought the same thing, only to later see their child's face on the side of a milk carton.

"Still nothing?" Jordie's mother asks the next morning when Jordie drops the phone handset back onto its base. Mrs. Cross is at the stove making oatmeal, the best way to start the day—hot, hearty and extremely low on the glycemic index.

"She's freaking out," Jordie says. At first, Mrs. Maugham's voice was just shaky. But it quickly devolved into something more liquid. It sounded to Jordie as if Mrs. Maugham was crying. "She thinks he's been in an accident or something. He's not answering her calls or her texts."

"If it was you or Carly, I'd be freaking out." Mrs. Cross shudders at the thought. "Have they called the police?"

"First thing this morning. He's officially a missing person." She can't quite believe it. Where is he? She can understand if he's angry with her for what she said—and with Ronan for showing up at the house and starting everything—and, because of that, doesn't feel like responding to her texts. But what does he have against his mom? Why is he acting like that to her?

"I still don't understand why he left the house," Mrs. Cross says. "He didn't say anything to you about where he was going?"

Jordie shakes her head but feels guilty, even though the gesture represents the truth. Derek took off sometime after Jordie more or less accused him of lying and theft. He didn't say anything about leaving. But she can't shake the idea that she's the reason he's gone. She's been thinking about it all night and has now concluded it's unlikely that Derek took the bracelet, despite what Ronan says he saw. Derek is an open guy—too open—and the look on his face was one of pure innocence. He can't hide anything— his feelings, what he did, what he didn't do—and people who can't hide anything can't lie. At least, they can't lie and get away with it. Can they?

No, they can't.

She is sure of it now. Derek isn't someone who can lie without setting off alarm bells. But now she's worried that after what she said, he decided to go home and get the bracelet he says he bought her for their anniversary (which isn't even an anniversary; how can anything be an anniversary after only one-sixth of an *annum*?), the one he said he was planning to give her on New Year's Eve, so that he can prove to her that whatever Ronan thought he saw, it wasn't the bracelet in question.

It had snowed the night before. Heavily. And it was cold. She'd felt the bite in the air in those few minutes outside with Ronan. What if something happened to Derek on the way home? What if he fell or was hit by a car? Or what if someone had mugged him or tried to rob him and he put up a fight? She finds it hard to imagine something like that happening in her neighborhood or his, but their neighborhoods aren't the whole town, and bad things happen everywhere. You just have to read the local paper to see what some citizens get up to in their spare time. It's a stereotype to think that muggings or worse happen only in LA or New York or Detroit.

It hits her like an iceball. She should tell Mrs. Maugham exactly what she's thinking. Or maybe she should tell the police. If they're looking for Derek, it will be helpful for them to know where he might have gone, which path he might have taken. She should definitely tell someone.

But first she wants to clear up once and for all the other thing that's been eating at her, the less important thing.

She knows where she put that bracelet, but it isn't there now. She's as close to positive now as she can be that Derek didn't take it. So where is it?

Unless it grew legs and walked away (as her mother would say), it must still be in her room. It only stands to reason.

Jordie goes back upstairs and begins one last methodical search for the bracelet Ronan gave her. She doesn't rip through her drawers like she did before. This time she searches them carefully, removing things one by one and putting them back in their places before moving on to the next drawer, the next piece of furniture, the next flat surface, the next patch of carpet.

"What're you looking for?" asks a voice at the door.

It's her sister, Carly, two years younger than Jordie, although you'd never know it from all the makeup she wears, not to mention the skanky clothes. Jordie can't imagine why her parents let her out of the house looking the way she does.

"None of your business." Jordie closes the second-to-bottom dresser drawer and opens the bottom one, although she isn't sure why. She keeps sweaters in that drawer; there's no way she would put anything valuable in there. She never has.

There is no bracelet.

"I know you're looking for something." Carly is leaning against the doorframe, her toes not quite touching the edge of carpet that marks the interior boundary of

Jordie's room. It's an irritating habit she picked up for those times when Jordie refuses her entry into the room. It's a habit made all the more alluring by the fact that it drives Jordie crazy and neither girl is allowed to close her door in the other's face. Privacy, yes. Rudeness, no.

"Well, since you're so smart, then you should already know what it is." Jordie slides the bottom drawer shut and stands with her hands on her hips, wondering where to turn next. She tries to visualize the last time she saw the bracelet. It's been months since she wore it, well before she and Derek started seeing each other. She closes her eyes for a moment and tries to picture the last time she had it on—or took it off.

She and Ronan had had a fight. That was it. Except it wasn't a fair fight—not in the sense of being two-sided anyway. Ronan was great with his fists. Put him up against another guy he was pissed at or who was pissed at him, and you'd see some genuine pugilistic combat. But put him against a girl whose main weapon—whose only weapon, by choice—was words, and all you got was silence. Like from a boulder. Or a wall. Like—it was so hard to tell, and that was the problem—from someone who didn't care.

She'd wanted to know what was wrong, why he was sulking around, why he didn't hand in his homework when it was stuff he could have done with his eyes closed, for God's sake, so why not take the twenty or thirty minutes or whatever it was and get it done and stop having all that grief rain down on him that only put everyone in a bad mood and screwed with their plans, which had to get canceled again because all of a sudden Mr. Atherly had had it up to *here* with him and had assigned him an essay that, *trust me, you don't hand this in first thing Monday, young man, and you are not, repeat, not passing this class in my lifetime, so put that in your pipe and smoke it.* Mr. Atherly, who never raised his voice to anyone, and who never, ever, said anything as asinine as *put that in your pipe and smoke it.* He must have been reliving something his father said to him thirty or forty years ago.

Of course, Ronan didn't answer. Instead, she got the stare. Then she got the shrug. Then she got the shift of his eyes away from her and off to something to the left, when all that was there was a brick wall, the exterior wall of the gym, in fact.

That's when it had dropped down on her like a tiny bird landing on her shoulder, as light as a puff of air but with a chirp that was loud and clear: You cannot communicate with this guy, Jordie. Sure, he's got amazing eyes and he's great to look at and has a great body. And you bet his ass is the best ass in jeans of any guy, bar none, in this whole school. And sure, he's got those soft lips and, boy, can he kiss. And those hands—Jesus, Mary and Joseph, talk about a burning bush. He's sweet, too, in a kind of inarticulate, semi-bashful way. And every now and then he says something that makes you sit up and take notice, like when her grandpa was gruff and cranky after having his heart attack, and Ronan said he didn't care how old someone was or how wise they seemed most of the time, he was pretty sure they were as afraid of dying as anyone else, even if it didn't seem that way to younger people. He said it with a fierceness she hadn't seen in him before. And then he said maybe it would be a good idea to go and see him, maybe try to cheer him up a little—something else he'd never done before. And they did go, and her grandpa liked Ronan. But that kind of thing didn't happen very often, whereas the stare, the shrug and the shift off to left field happened all the time, and she couldn't get a word out of him about why.

Before she could say what was on her mind, he broke up with her. Just like that. "This isn't working for me," he said.

She went home. She went up to her room, in tears, of course, because even though she was angry with him, she was also hurt. She had stood right in front of the mirror on top of her dresser and looked at herself. She remembered that. She remembered asking herself, Am I the one who's crazy, or is it him? Then, yes, she had slipped off the bracelet and held it. She had opened the top drawer and she had set the bracelet inside, in the tray where she kept her other bracelets, the two good ones—one from her parents and one from her grandmother—and the two matching pairs of earrings that went with them.

Her eyes pop open now. She slides the drawer out. Then, slowly, she turns toward the door.

"Have you been in my things?"

The movement is almost imperceptible. Almost, but not quite. Jordie catches the flash of tension in her sister's body against the wooden doorframe.

"Me? You think I'm crazy?"

Jordie watches her, counting the seconds until her twitchy little sister does exactly what Jordie expects her to do: she peels herself off the doorframe, as if she's suddenly bored by what's going on in Jordie's room.

Jordie is on her before she takes a full step. She wraps her hand around Carly's bony upper arm and yanks her into the room. She closes the door and flattens herself against it so that Carly has no way out.

"You were, you little rat. You were in here. You took it, didn't you?"

"I don't know what you're talking about." Carly thinks she's quick-witted when, really, she's just predictable. Well, Jordie isn't going to let her get away with that.

"I'm going to tell Mom," Jordie says. "She told you last time that if you came in my room and took something without permission again, she was going to ground your sorry little ass for a month. You remember that, right?"

Carly bucks up. "You need proof."

Sassy little bitch. "You're the only person besides Mom and Dad who has access to my room. You're the only person besides Mom who knows where I keep my good jewelry. And you're the only person, period, who has a reason to take my things, never mind a history

of actually taking them. I'm talking about the court
of Mom, Carly, not a court of law. If I go down there
and talk to her right now, you'll be spending the next
month staring at the four walls of your room. Is that
what you want?"

As hoped, Carly breaks.

"If you're talking about that bracelet that Ronan gave
you, I don't see what the big deal is," she says.

"Is it yours?" Jordie shrieks at her. "Is it?"

Carly cowers, her eyes on the door. Jordie allows
herself to smile.

"I bet if I yell a little louder, Mom will come up."

"Okay," Carly says, cowed and exasperated. "Okay, so
big deal—I took it."

"I want it back." Jordie thrusts out her hand. "Now."

Carly bites her lips.

"Now means now, Carly."

"Um…that could be a problem."

"Because?"

"Because I kind of gave it to someone."

"Kind of?"

"Okay, so I did. I gave it away. You dumped the guy.
You said you never wanted to see him again. I don't know
why you even kept the bracelet. It's not like you were ever
going to wear it."

Jordie can barely contain the rage that is burbling
inside her. "I never wear the bracelet Grandma gave me."
It's too clunky and old-fashioned, although she would

never say that to her grandmother, or to her mother, for that matter. "Are you planning to give it away too?"

"That's different."

"I want that bracelet back, Carly."

No answer.

"Who did you give it to?"

No answer.

Jordie reaches for the doorknob behind her.

"Wait!" Carly shouts. "Tasha. I gave it to Tasha."

"Call her right this minute and tell her you want it back."

Carly hesitates, swirling some words around in her mouth before finally spitting them out. "She might not give it back," she says finally.

"Because?"

No answer.

"Carly, because…?" Jordie's voice is uncomfortably loud for her sister.

"Because I sort of sold it to her."

"You *sold* my bracelet?" Since when did her little sister grow such a greedy and larcenous soul? "So give her back the money."

"I spent it."

"Tough. Let me put it this way, Carly. You *stole* my bracelet and then sold it. She bought *stolen* property. If I report this to the cops—and don't think I won't—she'll have to give it back, and then she'll drop you like a hot potato and you won't have any friends and maybe I'll even decide to press charges." Her voice is getting louder and louder. "Do you get what I'm saying to you?"

"I get it, I get it."

"Call Tasha or go over to her house and get that bracelet and bring it back to me right now. I'm giving you an hour. After that, I'm going to Mom."

"She's in Florida. She won't be back until the day after tomorrow." A look of defiance appears in her eyes. "What was Ronan doing here the other night?"

Jordie stares at her sister, gives her a real stinkeye.

"Either I have that bracelet in my hand by bedtime the day after tomorrow or you are in such a deep and smelly pit of trouble that you'll never see daylight again. You got that?"

Carly, eyelinered eyes wide with apprehension, nods and swallows hard. Jordie steps away from the door to let her out of the room.

Eight

While Jordie is issuing threats, Regis Minnow, forty-seven, father of two young boys and owner of a black Labrador named Barney, purchased for and named by said boys, is being yanked along a snow-covered pathway, his arm straight out ahead of him, then to his right, then in front again but tracking left, then momentarily to his left as Barney sniffs the environs for anything of interest. Ten months ago, when Regis and his wife, Melanie, brought the dog home, Regis took Barney's lively curiosity as a sign of intelligence. It was an understandable error—Regis had never owned a dog before. His mother refused to even consider having a defecating animal in the house. Since then, however, Regis, a teacher of American literature at the community college, has done his reading. It's possible that as one-year-old Labs go, Barney is blessed with intelligence. But, all the books caution, young dogs of Barney's size generally consist of two key elements: the body of an athlete and the brain of a two-year-old child. The athleticism tends to wane over time, as it does in humans. That two-year-old brain never really matures. Barney yanks and pulls, bounds forward and stops suddenly, jerking Regis to an arm-wrenching halt, at more or less the same places every single day. These are usually places where other dogs have peed or defecated, and nothing can move Barney from those spots until he's stuck his nose deep into the once-wet or, at the very least, moist ground and inhaled deeply a few times. Perhaps if Regis were twenty-seven instead of forty-seven, or if he'd given up tennis at the first sign of a deteriorating shoulder joint, he wouldn't mind. But today, as bone-chilling cold as it is, he minds a great deal. That's why, not even a mile into their walk, Regis bends down and snaps the leash off Barney's collar and doesn't give a second thought to where the dog might go after it bounds off the path and plunges into knee-deep snow.

Barney is out of sight a minute later. Three minutes after that, the barking starts—loud, deep, continuous. Barking that demands attention.

"Barney! Come!" Regis bellows, his hands cupped around his mouth to create a megaphone effect.

The barking doesn't let up for so much as a second.

"Barney!"

The dog probably can't hear him above the sound of his own throaty voice.

Goddamn it, Regis thinks, glancing down at his ankle-high boots.

"Barney! Come!"

If anything, the barking gets louder. What if the beast is injured? What if he's walked into some kind of trap? There were some set out in the area last winter by a kid who said he was trying to catch squirrels. He didn't say what he was planning to do with them once he'd caught them. The kid was twelve; the cops had let him off with a warning. Ten years from now he'll probably be a serial killer, Regis thinks. That's how they get started—with small animals. They work their way up the food chain from there.

Regis bends and tucks the bottoms of his jeans into the tops of his boots. The first step off the trail lands him shin-deep in show. A half-dozen more steps and he's almost knee-deep. This had better be good, he thinks, as he flounders after Barney's footprints.

He finds the Lab a hundred yards from the trail in a dense stand of pine. The dog is circling a tree, barking nonstop. Regis readies the leash to snap onto the dog collar.

"Barney!"

The dog reminds him of a windup toy, the way he goes around and around and around. Regis reaches for his collar and attaches the leash. Only then does he see what's got the dog going. There's someone under the tree—someone who isn't moving.

Nine

With the bracelet more or less under control—she isn't even sure how it has become her top priority—Jordie turns her mind back to Derek. It's been two full days now that he's been missing. She can understand his not returning her phone calls or texts, but not answering his mom or dad? What kind of sense does that make? Mrs. Maugham must be right. Something must have happened to him. The more she thinks about it, the more convinced Jordie is that he left because of her, because of what she said. She feels guiltier than ever.

She still isn't sure when he left the house. She's checked with her parents and her sister. No one heard him. And as far as she can tell from her twice-daily phone calls to his parents, the police haven't located anyone who saw him that night. If only he'd stayed downstairs on the pull-out couch in Jordie's basement. If only...

But he didn't stay down there. He left the house and went off somewhere. There are two possibilities that make sense to her. One, he was angry at what she said and went out for a walk sometime in the night, and something happened to him. Or, two, he went home to get the bracelet he bought her for their anniversary, to prove to her that what Ronan saw wasn't the bracelet he gave Jordie. If he left for the first reason, she has no idea where he might have gone. But if he left for the second reason, well, not only does she know where he went, but she knows the route he most likely followed. But she hasn't told the Maughams this, because she hasn't wanted to admit to them, or to anyone else, including herself, that this might be all her fault. She hasn't told anyone about the argument she had with Derek. But she has information that no one else has. Doesn't she have a duty to tell someone?

The easiest thing would be to pick up the phone and call the police: I'm Derek Maugham's girlfriend (no need for anyone to know that was about to change) and I'm pretty sure he went home that night to get something. But easiest isn't always best. If she's responsible for his leaving the safety of her basement and somehow coming to harm, she has to confess to that. And the best person to confess to is his parents. It seems only right somehow, although she can't explain exactly how.

She pulls on her coat and boots. She wraps a scarf around her neck. She plops a hat on her head and tugs gloves onto her hands. She trudges out into the snow. She walks to the edge of town and through the metal gateway that signals an entrance to the old rail line, now a hiking trail that runs along the north end of town and through the meadows on the right-of-way to the next town. She scans both sides of the trail on her way, looking for, hoping to see, Derek emerging from the woods, waving: *Here I am!* She can see that others have been here, notices hundreds of deep footprints, knee-high, some of them thigh-high, in the snow at the bottom of the slope on one side of the trail. She sees animal tracks too. The police have been here. Have there also been volunteers? Have there been dogs? Have they found anything?

She quickens her pace, and soon she is marching up the hill that leads to Derek's house, the hill they have flown down on the dented metal Magic Saucer that belongs to his dad, and that his dad used to sled on back when he was a kid. First she sees the snow-covered roofs of two houses, the Diehls' on the north side of the road and the Maughams' on the south side, their smoking chimneys peeking through. Next come windows and porch roofs and—cop cars. There are cop cars in front of Derek's house.

She runs.

She's panting by the time she reaches the two squad cars parked in the road between the two houses.

Mr. and Mrs. Maugham are out there. So is Lieutenant Diehl—*Mr.* Diehl, he's been telling everyone to call him lately; Jordie can't get used to thinking of him that way. She races to Mrs. Maugham.

"What's going on? Did something happen? Did they find Derek?"

Mrs. Maugham's face is a quilt of hurt, worry, surprise, despair. But there are no tears.

"I think it's about Elise Diehl. But they haven't said what yet."

Jordie lets out the beginning of a sigh of relief. She has heard—everyone has heard—that Mrs. Diehl is missing too. If she and Derek had anything in common, it would seem like the beginning of an epidemic or maybe of some old black-and-white science fiction movie. But Mrs. Diehl's disappearance is not unusual. There's nothing peculiar about it. She wandered off. She's been wandering for some time now.

Jordie still can't get over it. She had Mrs. Diehl for sixth grade. Half the kids in town have had her. She was the best teacher ever—fun, funny, sharp and fair. That was the thing kids loved about her. She was fair. She gave everyone a chance. She used to say that every person had a gift. But so what—lots of grownups say that, right? Right. But the thing is, Mrs. Diehl not only believed it, but also found that gift and helped its bearer recognize and celebrate it. She was the one who had made Jordie see that she didn't have to settle for what her parents had settled for, that she could get to college and make something of herself. She was the one who had encouraged Craig Harlan when he scribbled those poems and stories— Craig, who was two years older than Jordie and was now doing a fine-arts degree clear across the country. She was the one who had bought new sneakers for Martin DeLuce when she saw how fast he was, putting him on track for where he was headed next fall: a first-string college on an athletic scholarship. Mrs. Diehl had made a lot of kids what they were today, and the whole time she had been making them, fate had been unmaking her. She had been slipping away. Early-onset Alzheimer's. Slow at first, so she just seemed forgetful. Then faster, so you couldn't have a conversation with her—not a real one anyway. And then came the wandering.

Jordie glances at the cops, at Sergeant Tritt huddled with Mr. Diehl. She's definitely not going to talk to them about Derek, not when everyone looks so serious. She looks instead at Mrs. Maugham.

"There's something I need to tell you about that night," she begins.

Mrs. Maugham takes her eyes off her neighbor.

"Derek and I had a sort of argument," Jordie says.

"Oh?" There is an archness to Mrs. Maugham's voice that startles Jordie, as if this confession is something the woman has been waiting for, as if she has suspected all along that Jordie is somehow to blame for her son's disappearance. "You never mentioned that."

"It wasn't a big deal. I mean, it wasn't like we were breaking up or anything." Jordie wants to make that clear right away, even if subsequent thinking on her part has more or less rendered the last statement a lie. "We didn't yell at each other or anything. We watched a movie afterward. But I think, on account of the argument, that Derek might have come home to get something that night."

"Come home? You mean here, to our house?" Mrs. Maugham frowns as she digests this piece of information, struggling, it seems, to make sense of it.

"Yes."

"But he's not here now. I looked." Her face drains of color. "Richard!"

Mr. Maugham, standing closer to the end of the driveway, turns his head.

"Richard, did you look in the basement?"

"The basement?" Jordie can see that Mr. Maugham is out at sea. He doesn't understand why his wife is asking him this. "What for?"

"For Derek."

Mr. Maugham's whole body turns now. "Derek's in the basement? What the hell is he doing down there?"

"It's the one place we didn't look." Mrs. Maugham is already being drawn to the house. "Maybe he fell down the stairs. Maybe someone broke in. Maybe—" She lets out a moan that attracts the attention of Diehl and the earnest police. Mr. Maugham is quick to reassure them that everything is okay, that his wife is just feeling the strain of worry about their son. He runs after her, and together they go through the side door of the house, headed, Jordie knows, for the basement. This wasn't what she meant at all. She's almost sorry that she came.

Across the street, Sergeant Tritt lays a hand on Diehl's shoulder.

"If it's any consolation," Tritt says, "they say freezing to death is painless. And in her condition..." He leaves the thought there and lets Diehl fill in the details.

He wonders if he should tell him the rest—that Elise's knuckles are crusted with blood, that his best guess is she tried to get in someplace warm, maybe tried to batter down a door or maybe knocked somewhere, somewhere deserted, so hard that she skinned her knuckles.

But maybe that's not what happened. He's seen Elise a couple of times in the past two months that Diehl has been on leave. She didn't know what she was doing half the time. Maybe she pounded her fists against a tree. Maybe she thought the tree was a person. It's possible. In any case, Diehl will see her knuckles himself soon enough. He will draw his own conclusions. Tritt starts to steer Diehl to one of the squad cars. But his cell phone interrupts him. He lifts it to his ear, stepping away from Diehl as he answers. He keeps walking and stands up the road in the snow, his back to everyone. It isn't long before he slips the phone into the pocket of his jacket. He beckons to one of the patrol officers.

"Take the lieutenant to the morgue and stay with him. Make sure he's okay."

The patrol officer nods.

"Everything okay?" Diehl asks Tritt.

"Another call. Nothing I can't handle. Look, Mike, Pete'll take care of you. I'll check in on you later, okay?"

Diehl is frowning, as if he senses something is wrong. But he lets Pete guide him to a patrol car and slides into the backseat. Still, he looks over his shoulder at Tritt as the car crunches over the snow on its way down the hill.

Tritt's boots squeak beneath him. He talks to the two patrol officers who remain, and they get into their car. They all drive away, leaving Jordie alone on the street and unsure what to do. The Maughams do not reappear. In the end, Jordie trudges home. It is dark by the time she gets there.

It's on the news that night—Elise Diehl has been found dead in the woods by the river that runs north from town. She is said to have wandered away from her family home in the middle of the night and been unable to find her way back. The news announcer recalls her as a popular elementary schoolteacher who has recently suffered from Alzheimer's disease. Her husband, local police lieutenant Mike Diehl, has no comment, and no announcement has been made yet about funeral or memorial services.

"So sad," Jordie's mother says. "Especially so soon after her father's passing."

"It's a cruel disease," Jordie's father says. One of his aunts is afflicted with the same disease and is in a nursing home. She recognizes no one, does not speak and cannot look after herself.

"She was the best teacher I ever had," Jordie says.

"I think she was already losing her mind when I had her," Carly chimes in. "She used to spend an awful lot of time looking for stuff that was right on her desk and asking kids if they were new." In fact, Mrs. Diehl retired from teaching the year after Carly was in her class. Her face lost its bright smile and cheerful glow after that and became slack and pale. Her eyes lost their sparkle. The few times that Jordie saw her around lately, before her father died, Mrs. Diehl seemed to look right through her, as if Jordie were a window.

"Poor Lieutenant Diehl," Jordie's mother says. "I heard he took a leave of absence to look after her. Her father was determined she not be institutionalized, you know. The lieutenant isn't that old. Heavens, she wasn't that old, especially to have such a terrible disease. I suppose he'll go back to work soon. I can't see a man like that staying cooped up in that house all alone."

The weather comes on the TV. More snow is forecast, which the weatherman is sure will make the ski-resort operators happy. Then it's on to *Wheel of Fortune*, which Jordie's mother watches every night, followed by *Jeopardy*.

Her father sits on the couch with her, but he is usually hidden behind a magazine or a newspaper, and by the time *Wheel* is half over, he is dozing. Jordie goes upstairs and lies on her bed. She could watch something on her computer. She could listen to some music. She could read—she likes to read, and she got some books for Christmas. But she does none of these things. Instead, she thinks about Ronan.

Ronan, not Derek who is missing. Or, rather, Ronan at first and then she thinks, What am I doing? Derek is missing. He's the one I should be thinking about. But her mind goes back to Ronan. She wonders what he is doing. She doesn't think he's seeing anyone else—she's pretty sure that if he was, she would have seen or heard something at school. For sure someone would have told her if he'd been seen with someone else. But that hasn't happened.

Does he miss her? Did he miss her for a while and then get over her? It drives her crazy that she wasn't able to decipher the look on his face when he was standing on her porch the other night. Did it bother him that Derek was there? Did it bother him that Derek was staying there for a few days? Ronan had never done that. Her parents, especially her mother, found him hard to warm up to. "He's so quiet," Mrs. Cross said on more than one occasion. "And the way he looks at a person—it's like he's thinking something that you're sure you don't want to hear."

Jordie knows this isn't true—or at least, she used to think she knew that. The reason she broke up with him:

she realized she didn't know what he was thinking, so it is more than merely possible that her mother was right. So why is Jordie thinking about him now? Why isn't she thinking about Derek? Why isn't she out looking for Derek?

Maybe she falls asleep with this idea in her head. Maybe that's why she wakes up early, intent on going out and looking for Derek. Despite the forecast, it hasn't snowed, so Jordie dresses and heads out to take once again the path Derek most likely took when he went home that night. Assuming he went home.

She walks slowly this time. Her eyes scan both sides of the trail as well as the trail bed. An hour passes and she is only halfway to the hill that leads up to Derek's house. Her eyes start to water from the strain of scrutinizing so much bright white surface snow. She wants to rest them, but clouds are already gathering to the north. Before too long they will fill the sky, and it will start to snow. She moves forward, keeping her pace slow, forcing her eyes to make the same movements on each side of the trail—straight ahead into the distance as far as she can see in front of the trees, then among the trees, a little to the right, a little to the left, straight ahead again. She is halfway up the slope behind Derek's house and about to give up when she sees it. It's off in the distance, among the trees, and it's only because she's up this high that it catches her eye, there, in a little clearing just barely visible from where she is. It's orange—Derek's scarf. She's sure of it.

The next minute she's just as sure it can't be Derek's scarf. His parents have been out looking for him. Some of their friends have been out. The police have been out. They have all probably tramped the same path Jordie is tramping now. There's no way they haven't seen what she is looking at now—seen it and investigated it and dismissed it as nothing of relevance. She's kidding herself if she thinks she's going to be the one to find him—here, at least. He must be somewhere else—someplace where no one has looked yet.

She raises a hand to shield her eyes and takes another look. There is definitely something there. It's possible that a dog or some other animal—a fox or maybe a coyote—has found him or at least his scarf and tugged at it, and maybe that's why it's there now. Maybe it wasn't there yesterday or the day before. Or it's possible the wind has blown the snow cover off it. Sure, there are a couple of ways—plausible ways—to explain how she is seeing a scarf no one saw before. She starts back down the hill.

Once she is off the rail trail, her legs plunge deep into the snow. Soon she is wading knee-high in the stuff. It's hard going. Sweat soaks into her T-shirt and her sweater before she makes it to the tree line. She's lost sight of the clearing but is doing her best to keep on course to where she is pretty sure it is. Soon she is wheezing like a lifelong smoker. The clearing is nowhere in sight. She must have veered off course. To find it, she will have to go back to the rail trail, climb the hill again and search the trees. It's almost too exhausting to contemplate. Overhead, more clouds have rolled in, and the sky has turned from blue to gray. She has to move fast. If she doesn't, the snow will start falling and will obliterate any trace of the orange she is sure she saw.

She turns to head back. Wait—what's that? A patch of white with no trees in it. She pumps her legs and arms, trying to push the snow out of her way as she urges her body toward it. She is gasping for breath. Jesus, she had no idea she was so out of shape. But there it is, a flash of orange. It's a scarf. It's Derek's scarf—she's ready to swear to it. She grabs it and lifts it. It comes up easily out of the snow. It is Derek's scarf, the same scarf he always wore, the scarf he was wearing the whole time he was staying at her house, the scarf he must have worn when he left the house that night because it was nowhere to be found in the basement or in the closet or on the hooks by the side door. It is definitely his scarf. There's no doubt in her mind. She stands in the clearing beside it and calls his name.

He doesn't answer.

Of course he doesn't answer.

She begins scooping the snow with her mittened hands, slowly at first, then frantically, as if she can still save him if he's down there. But Derek isn't there.

She calls Derek's name again, praying harder than she has prayed for almost anything that he will answer, that what everyone fears isn't true, that he is fine.

No one answers.

But he was here sometime in the past couple of days; that much is clear. He was here and somehow he lost his scarf. She drops it, pulls her phone out of her pocket, locates the phone number for the local police and calls them.

Ten

Three quarters of an hour later, Jordie stands shivering on the rail trail. After she made the call but before she retreated to the trail, she tromped a gigantic X in the snow where she found the scarf. The exertion made her sweat. The sweat has dried and chilled her throughout. But she stays where she is, waiting for the police.

Finally, here they come, two officers in winter hats and heavy coats and boots. They're coming down the hill near the Maughams' house. Jordie runs forward to meet them. She tells them about the scarf and explains that the last time she saw Derek, he had it with him. She tells them about him leaving her house that night and not coming back. Then she leads them back up the hill a little ways—"You can't see it unless you're at least halfway up"—and points to the flash of orange and the X. "That's his scarf. And that's where I found it. I didn't find him though."

One of the cops goes back down to the bottom, jumps off the trail and starts wading toward the clearing. The other one takes Jordie's name and contact information. He sets out after his partner.

Jordie is trembling so violently that her teeth are chattering, but she stays where she is, waiting. She loses sight of the police. And of the time. It seems as if they are in that clearing forever.

"Jordie? Jordie, is that you?"

She turns and looks up the hill. It's Mr. Maugham. He is standing near the top, looking down at her.

"Is that the police down there?" he calls to her. "What are they doing?"

Jordie realizes he must be able to see them from where he is. She doesn't know what to say. Mr. Maugham starts down the hill toward her.

"What are you doing out here?" he asks. "Good Lord, you're shaking—" He breaks off when one of the police officers appears through the trees. He is talking on his phone as he trudges toward them. "What's that he's carrying?" he asks. He squints. "Is that—that looks like Derek's." Jordie knows he means the scarf.

Mrs. Maugham comes scurrying down the path, her coat flying open behind her, and Jordie realizes she must have seen something from the house.

"What's going on?" Her breath accumulates in white puffs in front of her face. "What are they doing out there? Is it Derek?" All of this is directed at her husband.

"They have Derek's scarf," Mr. Maugham says. He hasn't once taken his eyes off the police officer who is wading through the snow toward them.

Mrs. Maugham peers at the young man in the blue parka, his face earnest, who is now climbing up the slope to the rail trail. He has the scarf in one hand and a small plastic bag in the other. There's something in it. Something small and round.

"Do you recognize this?" The police officer holds up the scarf.

"It's Derek's." Mrs. Maugham grabs for it, startling the officer and forcing him to whisk it back out of her reach.

"Please, ma'am," he says. "It's evidence." He holds out the plastic bag. "What about this?"

Mrs. Maugham thrusts her head forward to take a closer look. "Is that a button?"

"Yes, ma'am. Do you recognize it?"

Mrs. Maugham stares at it and shakes her head slowly. "Derek doesn't have anything with that kind of button on it. I'd know if he did."

Jordie doesn't doubt this. Unlike herself, Derek isn't required to do any housework. Yard work, yes. Raking, shoveling, trundling out garbage and recycling containers—absolutely. Dishes, laundry, ironing, mending—uh-uh. Mrs. Maugham insists on doing all of that for her one and only child.

"What about you, miss?"

Jordie is staring so intently at the button that it takes her a few seconds to register that the police officer is speaking to her.

"Have you seen this button before?"

Jordie shakes her head. "No."

"You said the scarf and the button are evidence," Mr. Maugham says slowly.

Mrs. Maugham looks at him. Her face blanches. "Oh my god. Did you find Derek? Is my son out there?"

The officer turns to Mr. Maugham. "Sir, could I ask you to take your wife up to the house? Someone will be up to talk to you shortly. I need to speak with this young lady." He nods at Jordie.

"Why?" Mrs. Maugham demands. "Why do you need to speak to *her*?"

"Please, ma'am. Sir?"

"I don't understand," Mrs. Maugham says to Jordie. "Why do they need to speak to you? Do you know where Derek is?"

Mr. Maugham puts an arm around his wife's shoulder. "Come on, Marsha." He starts to guide her away from Jordie and the officer, but she won't let herself be removed from the scene.

"What did you do to him?" Mrs. Maugham's eyes bore into Jordie. "What did you do to Derek?"

Jordie feels her cheeks turn hot in the frigid morning air. The police officer's eyes linger on her for longer than feels comfortable.

"Marsha, please." Mr. Maugham presses his lips to his wife's ears and whispers something. Only then does she allow him to walk her up the hill to the house.

The police officer waits until they are out of earshot before pulling out his memo book and a pen.

"Now then," he says, "tell me again how you happened to find this scarf."

Jordie's feet are blocks of ice. Her face is so stiff from the cold that she can barely form words. But she stands where she is, on the path, and watches as more police officers show up, and then a dog, and they all wade into the deep snow and disappear from sight. She knows that if she were to look up the hill and could see the Maughams' kitchen window, she would see their two faces at it. Mr. and Mrs. Maugham are doing the same thing Jordie is—they are watching and waiting, unable to stop themselves. Perhaps, like Jordie, they are praying. Perhaps they are praying that Derek will be found. Or, in the case of Mrs. Maugham, perhaps praying that he will not be found, at least not in the way that she dreads he will be.

The air grows colder. A few snowflakes drift down from the heavens. Then more. Pretty soon the air is thick with large, fluffy flakes, the kind you can catch on your mitten, the kind you can look at and see for yourself that no two are alike. The police must be cursing. Every flake, every flurry, covers some minute spot out there and potentially obliterates some tiny piece of the puzzle they need to fit together to get to the answer of what happened to Derek. The flakes of snow become a veneer. The veneer becomes a layer one millimeter thick. The millimeter becomes a centimeter. The air is thick with snow, so thick that Jordie isn't sure at first that she is seeing what she thinks she is seeing—figures, white figures, coming out of the trees and making their way slowly toward the rail trail. There are two of them. One of them raises a hand. At first Jordie thinks he is waving at her, which makes no sense—why would he? Then she sees someone else coming down the trail—a man in a long coat. He heads into the deep snow and meets one of the snow-covered figures. They turn and go back the way he came. The second figure, a police officer, climbs to the trail and heads up the hill. On his way, he meets two more people. They are carrying a stretcher.

Jordie continues to wait.

She waits until the two men with the stretcher disappear behind the dense curtain of falling snow. She waits until they reappear thirty or more minutes later, walking more slowly now, carrying the stretcher between them, one in front, the other behind, and something lumpish on the stretcher between them. Jordie holds her breath as they stumble up the slope onto the trail and then carry their burden up the path. More police officers appear out of the snow. So does the man with the long coat. They all go up the hill, leaving Jordie in the silence of the falling snow. She waits until everyone vanishes and then she heads in the opposite direction, away from the Maughams' house, back down the path the way she came, barely feeling her feet the whole way, until she is home.

Eleven

At six o'clock that night, just as Mrs. Cross is about to put a chicken pot pie and green salad on the table and pull some biscuits from the oven, someone rings the doorbell. Mr. Cross, seated in the living room and therefore closest to the door, heaves himself to his feet and goes to answer. Deep, masculine voices can be heard. Mr. Cross calls his elder daughter to the door. Mrs. Cross, curious, follows her. Carly hovers in the doorway between the kitchen and the front hall.

"Jordie, you remember Sergeant Tritt," Mr. Cross says.

Behind Jordie, Mrs. Cross says, "Hello, Neil. What brings you here on a night like this?"

Art Cross and Neil Tritt are both members of the local curling club. They play against each other regularly and are so evenly matched that it's anyone's guess who will come out on top on any given night.

"He wants to talk to Jordie about Derek," Mr. Cross says.

"I'd like you to come down to the police station, Jordie," Tritt explains. "You can bring your dad with you if you'd like."

"Why?" Mrs. Cross demands. Normally, she is quiet and deferential with authority figures. But when her daughters are involved, her lamblike nature vanishes and she takes on the ferocity of a mama lion. "What's going on, Neil? What has she done?"

"We just need to ask her a few questions, Celia," Tritt says.

Jordie reaches for her coat on the hook by the door.

"Jordie, what's this all about?" her mother asks.

"It's Derek," she says. "They found him."

"Found him?"

Tritt glances at Mr. Cross. "I can drive you both, or you can come in your own car."

"We'll follow you." Mr. Cross reaches for his coat.

"It's okay, Dad," Jordie says. "You don't have to come with me. Why don't you stay and have supper?"

But he is buttoning his coat. Jordie wishes he would stay put, but she knows he won't. She can't blame him. She supposes that if she had a daughter and her daughter were wanted for questioning by the police, she would insist on staying with her.

"Jordie?"

"It's okay, Mom."

"Call me, Art," Mrs. Cross says. "Let me know what's happening."

Jordie and her father follow Tritt out into the night. Tritt gets into his car, which is parked at the curb, and waits, engine idling, while Jordie and her father climb into their car. Her father backs out of the driveway and heads to the business district of town. Tritt follows. On the way, Mr. Cross questions his daughter.

"Do you know why they want to talk to you?"

"About Derek."

"But why you?"

Jordie gives her father a look and shakes her head.

"Well, I knew him pretty well, Dad. He was at our house before he disappeared. And—" Here she hesitates. "I guess you could say I'm sort of responsible for him being found."

"Oh?" Her father, who is concentrating on the road because the snow is still falling hard, steals a glance at her.

"I was out for a walk today, and I saw something. It turned out it was Derek's scarf. The police took it from there."

"So when they say they found Derek…"

"He's dead." Jordie is surprised that she can say this without choking up or bursting into tears. "I saw them take him away."

Her father reaches for her and squeezes her hand.

"I'm sorry, honey."

They are silent the rest of the way to the police station.

When they get there and her father has to drive around to find a cleared spot to park in, Jordie thinks she will go crazy. She wants to go right in and get started. But Mr. Cross insists that she stay with him. They leave the car together and enter the police station, where Tritt, coatless now, is waiting. He ushers them past the desk sergeant and to the back of the station, guiding them into a small windowless room, its cinder-block walls painted a dull green.

"Thanks for coming, Jordie," Tritt says.

Mr. Cross glances at these new surroundings. "Does my daughter need an attorney, Neil?"

Tritt smiles. "Not at all." He turns to Jordie. "Sorry about the accommodations, but it is a police station."

"It's okay," Jordie says. She hesitates and doesn't sit until Tritt pulls out a chair for her.

"If you'll just wait here," he says, "we'll be with you in a minute."

We?

Jordie's father sits down beside her. They wait in silence until someone appears in the door. It's Lieutenant Diehl. Jordie's dad jumps to his feet.

"Mike, I wasn't expecting to see you here. We heard about Elise. I'm so sorry."

Diehl nods his thanks. He looks across the table at Jordie and asks her how she is.

"I'm okay, I guess," she says. "You know, under the circumstances." Then, following her father's lead and the nudgy expression in his eyes, she adds, "Mrs. Diehl was the best teacher I ever had. I'm sorry for your loss, sir."

Diehl lets go a shuddery sigh as he pulls out a chair across the table from Jordie and her dad and sinks down.

"Thank you," he says. "I appreciate that. But the truth is, I lost Elise a long time ago. Alzheimer's is a terrible thing. I hope you never have to go through it with anyone you love." He lays a file folder on the table in front of him but doesn't open it. "Now then, Jordie, do you know why you were asked to come down here tonight?"

"Because of Derek. Because I know him so well."

"That's right," Diehl says.

Mr. Cross is frowning. Sometimes Jordie thinks it's his default expression and that everything else, every wry look, every grimace, every rare and precious smile, is meted out on some kind of miserly quota system, as if he's afraid he'll use them up before his time on earth is finished.

"Are you investigating this, Mike?"

"I am."

"I thought you retired."

"I took a leave." There's a flicker of annoyance in his eyes. It seems to Jordie he doesn't take well to his interview being sidetracked by personal questions. "After her father died, Elise needed a lot of care—more than I could give her while I was holding down the job. But now—" He lets a moment of silence carry the rest. "And the Maughams live across the street from me."

Mr. Cross nods and says nothing.

"Now then, Jordie," Diehl says, "I need you to tell me about Derek."

"Did you talk to his parents?" Surely they know more than she does.

"I did. And I'll be talking to a lot of other people too— kids at school, teachers, anyone who can tell me anything that might help us figure out what happened to Derek."

"What did happen to him?" Mr. Cross asks. "Was it an accident?"

"I'm afraid not." Diehl's eyes are hard on Jordie. "It looks like he was murdered."

"Murdered?" Mr. Cross's eyes are wide with incredulity. "You must be kidding! Who would murder a kid like that?"

"How do you mean?" Diehl asks.

"Well, I mean, he was a nice boy. Never any trouble that I could see. He was staying at our house while his parents were away and was never a bit of trouble...you know, for a teenage boy staying at his girlfriend's house, if you know what I mean."

Jordie feels herself blush.

"I can't imagine who would kill that boy," Mr. Cross finishes.

"That's what we aim to find out," Diehl says.

"How did he die?" Jordie chooses her words carefully, but even so, her voice catches on the last word. Even though she saw his lumpish form on the stretcher, she still can't believe that's what it's come down to. Someone killed Derek.

"Blunt force trauma," Diehl says.

"A blow to the head," Tritt explains. "We're waiting on the postmortem to find out if he died immediately or if he was left out there in the cold and the snow to die."

Jordie's heart seizes up. Someone hit Derek on the head and left him to die in the cold and dark and snow.

"So, given that you knew him well and that he was staying with you the day before he went missing, we need to talk to you," Diehl says. "But first there are some details I have to get out of the way." He tells her that because she is only sixteen, a minor, she has certain rights, such as the right not to talk to the police if she doesn't want to.

"Of course she wants to," her father says. "Don't you, Jordie?"

Jordie nods.

Also that she has the right to have a parent or some other adult present while she talks to the police.

"Done," her father says.

That she's not under arrest, that she's free to leave at any time, but that anything she says can be used in a subsequent court proceeding.

"What is it you want to ask her?" her father asks.

Diehl ignores him. "You understand these rights, Jordie?"

"Yes."

He opens the file folder, slides a paper across the table to her and tells her to initial where he has puts *X*s and to sign at the bottom of the page. She skims the paper as she initials the boxes; it says exactly what he has already told her, and her initials and signature show that she understands and agrees.

"Derek's parents say that Derek didn't go with them to see his grandmother last weekend," Diehl says. "Instead, he stayed behind to be with you. Is that right?"

"You already know he did," Mr. Cross says. "You just said so yourself."

Diehl shoots a look of annoyance at Jordie's father. "I was talking to Jordie."

Mr. Cross bridles, but he doesn't speak.

"How long did Derek stay at your house, Jordie?" Diehl asks.

"All weekend. From Friday when his parents left until Monday morning. Or Sunday night. I'm not sure."

"Was anyone else there?"

Another odd question. Her dad has already said that Derek was no trouble, making it clear that at least he was there with them.

"My parents. And my sister."

"Were you all there the whole time?"

"Well, no. I mean, we were all there for supper on Friday. And then Carly—my sister—and Derek and I watched a movie downstairs. On Saturday, Derek and I went to the mall. I don't know what everyone else was doing. We went out for pizza and brought back some movies to watch. My parents were out."

"We were at the curling club," Mr. Cross says.

"And Carly was at a friend's house. She slept over."

"So it was just you and Derek at your house?" He's peering at her as if the answer she gives to this question means something, that it will reveal something about her or her trustworthiness.

"Yes," she says. She glances at her dad. "We didn't do anything we weren't supposed to." Unless her parents expected them to act like brother and sister, that was true. They did a bunch of other stuff, but none of it was wrong, and none of it was actual sex.

"What about Sunday?"

"I slept in. I guess Derek did too."

"You guess?"

"He slept in the basement."

"He got up about ten," her father says. "Helped me clear the driveway and then went next door and shoveled Mrs. Drake's walk for her. Like I said, he was a good kid."

Jordie rolls her eyes. Every time her dad calls Derek a good kid, even if it sounds like an innocent compliment, she knows better. What he means is that Derek was a good kid especially in comparison to Ronan.

"Was he having trouble with anyone?" Diehl asks. "Did he have any enemies, maybe at school or on the hockey team he played on?"

"No," Jordie says.

"No?" Her father's frown deepens. "How can you say that?"

"Because it's true." She's furious with her father for interrupting her. Diehl is asking her questions, not him.

"Is it, Jordie?" Diehl asks.

"Yes. He was a good guy. He didn't have enemies."

"He never argued with anyone? Never got into a shoving match or a fight? Nobody had a grudge against him?"

"Yes," her father says at the exact same time she says, "No." Father and daughter glare at each other. Then calmly, keeping her voice steady, Jordie turns to Tritt and says, "You told me I have the right to have a parent here, but that doesn't mean I have to, does it?"

"Jordie!" Mr. Cross can see where this is going, and he doesn't like it.

She refuses to look at him. "Does it?"

"No, it doesn't," Tritt says.

"Then I would like my dad to leave."

"Now listen here, Jordie—"

"If it will help us get the information we need, I think it might be a good idea, Art," Tritt says.

"And I say it's a bad idea. I'm her parent."

"She has the right not to have you present, Art." Tritt's expression is one of reasonableness. He leans forward slightly, his eyes fixed on Mr. Cross. "They were dating. You were seventeen once, Art. You went out with pretty girls like Jordie here. And I bet there were things about those relationships that you wouldn't have wanted to talk about with your old man in the room. Am I right?" Her father refuses to concede the point. "The Maughams have lost their son. Imagine it was you and Celia. Imagine something had happened to Jordie. You'd want us to get to the truth, wouldn't you? You wouldn't want anything to interfere with that, would you?"

Her father doesn't answer; he just stares across the table and then, still silent, pushes back his chair and gets up.

"I'll be outside," he says. He doesn't look at Jordie. He's angry with her, but she doesn't care. Tritt gets it. There are things she doesn't want to discuss with her father sitting right there. Plenty of things.

Tritt and Diehl wait until he is out of the room. Tritt gets up and closes the door and then sits down again. Jordie is glad of the pause. She knows exactly what her father is thinking about, and she bets that no matter what she says, Diehl will talk to him later and find out. But her father only sees things from a distance. She sees them close up. If she stays calm, if she doesn't panic and doesn't think for a second what her father might or might not say, it could be okay.

"Did Derek have any enemies, Jordie? Was anyone mad at him about anything?"

"No."

"Your dad seems to have other ideas about that."

"My dad thinks there was something between Derek and a guy I used to go out with."

"Was there?" Diehl asks.

"No. Like I said, Derek wasn't that kind of person. He never had any trouble with anyone. Even on his hockey team. He never fought—ever. That's one of the reasons my dad liked him."

"And if we were to talk to your father?"

Jordie answers promptly, even though she wishes she had time to think. She decides on the truth.

"I don't know. Maybe my dad knows something I don't. But I doubt it. Derek told me everything." Derek told her too much. "If Derek had any trouble with anyone, I would know about it."

"Okay," Diehl says. "So, Sunday, it sounds like Derek got up before you and helped your dad clear the driveway."

"And Mrs. Drake's. See what I mean? Parents just eat that stuff up."

"You're not saying it was an act, are you?"

No, she was not. "It was genuine. Like I said, Derek was a nice guy. Parents and teachers really liked him."

"What about you?"

"Me?" She tries not to show how blindsided she is by the question. "He was my boyfriend. I liked him a lot."

"What did the two of you do on Sunday after you got up?"

"I helped my mom make brunch—waffles and syrup." Her mom adored Derek too. She went all out whenever he came over. "We ate. Derek and Carly cleared the table and did the dishes. Then we went outside and fooled around in the snow for a while. Then cocoa and supper and TV. We played Rock Star."

"And after that?"

"After that?"

"Derek went home that night, correct?" Tritt says.

Jordie frowns. How does he know that?

"Mrs. Maugham told us that you told her you were pretty sure Derek went home that night to get something," Tritt explains.

"Did you go with him?" Diehl asks.

Jordie shakes her head. "I didn't even know he was going."

"Then how did you know he went home? Did you see him leave your house?"

Again she shakes her head. "I figured out later that that's what he must have done. He said he had a present for me. I think—well, I thought—he might have gone home to get it."

"Mrs. Maugham also says you told her the route you thought Derek took," Diehl says. "How did you know that?"

"It's the way he usually goes."

"We searched the area behind his house. We didn't find anything. How did you know where to look?"

"I guess I just got lucky."

Diehl leans forward. "Are you sure you weren't with him that night, Jordie?" His eyes are drilling into her.

"No. I mean, I wasn't with him." She wishes he would stop looking at her like that. Jesus, what does he think? Does he think she had something to do with it? Does he think *she* killed Derek? "I was at home. I was asleep when he left the house. I didn't know he was gone until the next morning."

"How about you and Derek?" Diehl asks.

Another question out of the blue. "What about us?"

"How were the two of you getting along? Did you fight at all—maybe a lovers' quarrel?"

What? Is he serious? "You don't seriously think *I* killed Derek, do you?"

"Did you?" Diehl asks. There is nothing joking in his voice. It's a serious question, and it unnerves her.

"No!" She wishes her father was back in the room with her. "I would never hurt Derek!"

"We have to ask these questions, Jordie," Tritt says, which is when Jordie sees what's going on. It's like a cop-show playbook—Diehl is bad cop, Tritt is good cop. These things really happen—at least, that's what Jordie is concluding. "We're just trying to get a fix on what happened."

"We were getting along just fine," Jordie says. So what if she and Derek had had a spat? That was nobody's business but their own—well, her own now.

"Is there anything else you can tell us about Derek?"

"Like what?"

"Who he hung around with. Where he liked to hang out. Anything at all, even if you don't think it's important or relevant."

She tells Diehl and Tritt who Derek's friends were—mostly the guys on the hockey team—and what he did in his spare time—mostly hanging out at the arena or on whatever ice he could find. He wasn't a complicated guy.

He loved to play hockey, watch hockey, talk hockey. He liked to eat; he had a teenage hockey player's appetite. And he liked her. He liked to be with her and touch her and have her touch him. But that part she leaves out. It has nothing to do with anything.

"Well," Diehl says finally, "I'd like to thank you for taking the time to come down here. And if you think of anything at all, Jordie, call me or Sergeant Tritt. You'll do that, right?"

She says she will.

Her father is waiting for her outside the small room. He's standing there, away from the wall, his coat over his arm, like a man waiting for a bus or a train. He waits for her to come to him and they walk out of the police station in silence. They don't talk on the way home.

Twelve

Midmorning the next day, there's a knock on her door. "Jordana, can I come in?"

Jordie slides off the bed to admit her mother, who is holding a tray on which she's put a cup of tea—it looks like green tea; if it is, it's spiked with organic honey—and two slices of buttered raisin toast.

"Are you okay, honey? I thought you might want something."

"Thanks, Mom." Jordie takes the tray and sets it on her bedside table. She sits on the bed again. Her mother hovers in the doorway. "I'm fine, Mom. Really."

"It's so terrible," Mrs. Cross says. "I can't imagine why anyone would want to do such a thing. His poor parents."

Jordie doesn't know what to say.

"Honey, we're going to Elise Diehl's funeral. Do you want to come?"

Jordie knows that going would be the right thing to do. But she shakes her head. The funeral may give her the opening she has been waiting for.

"Are you sure?" her mother says. "You always liked her."

Jordie turns watery eyes on her mother. "Derek is dead, Mom. I'm going to have to go to that funeral, which is something I never in a million years thought I would ever have to do. Please don't make me go to another one. I'll send a card to Lieutenant Diehl. I promise."

Mrs. Cross hesitates. She had the kind of upbringing that stressed social and community obligations. She remembers her father telling her on more than one occasion, *Always go to the funeral.* But her daughter's boyfriend has just been found dead in the woods. According to the police, he's been murdered. Maybe Jordie is right. Maybe one funeral is the most anyone can expect under the circumstances.

"We'll be gone for a couple of hours. If you need me—"

"I'll be fine, Mom."

"—you can always call."

Jordie nods. She wishes her mother would go.

But she doesn't go. "Do you want me to find out when Derek's funeral is?" she asks.

"I'm sure his parents will tell me," Jordie says. She feels almost guilty that she isn't nearly as upset as her mother is. She supposes that tells her something, either about her own temperament or about her feelings for Derek. She feels guilty about that too. She was going to break up with him. Yes, he was a sweet guy. Yes, he was kind and attentive and thoughtful. But did she love him? Maybe she would have if she hadn't already experienced the head-over-heels whirlwind-tornado-cyclone-hurricane of emotions that couldn't have been anything else but genuine, passionate, true and what she had believed at the time was timeless love with Ronan.

"Well then." Her mother is still in the doorway, still hovering, probably wondering what she can do to make everything better. She's that kind of mom, the kind who can't bear to see her children sad or hurt or wounded or upset, the kind who believes that if she says or does the right thing, it will have the magical effect of a kiss on a bruise, it will make everything better, make it whole again, banish whatever pain her children have suffered, as if suffering is operated by an on-off switch that only she can throw.

"Thanks for the tea, Mom. It's just what I wanted."

Her mother smiles. Her work done, she withdraws, closing the door carefully and silently.

Jordie sinks back against the pillow to wait. She hears the murmur of her parents' voices as they dress for the funeral. She hears Carly ask if anyone has seen her black sweater. She hears Carly again: "How come I have to go and Jordie gets to stay home?"

"Because of Derek," their mother says. That's it, the whole explanation. Maybe there will be more outside in the car. Or maybe Carly is finally—praise the Lord—old enough to understand that treating one's children equally does not always mean making them do the exact same thing.

Jordie hears her parents and Carly down in the front hall as they pull on coats and boots, scarves, hats and gloves. She hears the front door open and close. She hears the key turn in the lock. Then…silence.

She gets up, goes into her parents' room at the front of the house and stands close enough to the window to watch as the car pulls out of the driveway and starts down the street, but far enough away that no one can see her. She waits a full five minutes after it goes around the corner and vanishes from sight. Then she races back to her room, changes out of her pyjamas and goes downstairs to get into her coat and boots.

Ronan's car isn't in his driveway. It isn't behind the hardware store either, which means he isn't working today. So Jordie heads down to the lake and trudges around the point, where all the big houses are, and then hikes along the shore toward the old part of town, the part that was settled back in the 1800s, where many of the houses are originals and where, so far, none have been torn down to make room for some hideous monster house. If someone even thought of it, they'd have a fight on their hands, because the local historical society is vocal, and even the Chamber of Commerce recognizes that history sells.

There's a stretch of lakefront between the point and the old town that in summer is a public beach and in winter is more or less deserted. It is here that Jordie spots a figure on the ice. It's Ronan, taller than ever in his hockey skates, dressed in black jeans and a black jacket, a black tuque on his head. He's pushing a snow shovel, skating behind it in a straight line, up and down, up and down, cleaning off something roughly the size and shape of a hockey rink. He doesn't see her until she is close enough to touch him and she speaks.

"Getting ready for a game?"

Ronan jumps. When he sees who it is, he doesn't smile.

"What are you doing here?" His tone and the look that goes with it irk her. They're supposed to convey indifference. Whether they reflect his true feelings is anyone's guess. But Jordie, remembering how she used to feel about him, is reluctant to accept that they do.

"Maybe I came to give you back the bracelet," she says. "You know, the one you gave me and that now you want me to return."

Aha! There's a flicker of emotion in his eyes. The only trouble is, she can't figure out which one. Hurt, maybe? Or anger?

"Uh-huh," he says. "Is that why you came?"

She has to admit that it isn't. "I haven't found it yet." Ronan wraps his hand around the shovel handle again. "But Derek didn't have it," she adds.

"That's what he told you, huh?" Spoken like she's an idiot to believe that.

"It happens to be true." She's annoyed that he would say something like that now, given what's happened. "You heard what happened to him, right?"

She's stunned when he shakes his head.

"You're kidding me!"

He leans on the shovel and stares deep into her eyes. "Are you going to tell me, or are you going to make me guess?"

"You really don't know?" She isn't sure if she believes him. It's been in the local paper. It's been on the news. "He was missing."

"Yeah? And?"

"And they found him, Ronan."

"So, he's not missing anymore. Problem solved, right?"

Jesus. She wants to slap him. How can he really not know?

"He's dead, Ronan. Derek is dead."

The surprise on his face strikes her as genuine. But is it? She wants to believe she would recognize deceit, but going out with Ronan has taught her how little she knows about him. She was blindsided when the relationship ended. It's the kind of thing any girl should have seen coming. But she didn't. She was no better at reading

Ronan at the end than she was at the beginning, when he stunned her by suddenly becoming interested in her, then friendly.

"Dead?" he says now.

Jordie nods. "You didn't have anything to do with it, did you, Ronan?"

"What?" Also genuine, at least on the surface. "Me? What are you talking about?"

"Where did you go after you left my house?"

"What are you, the cops?"

"Just tell me, Ronan."

"You think I killed your boyfriend?"

"Did you?"

They stare at each other, both of them looking shocked by the words that have just come out of Jordie's mouth. Is she really accusing Ronan of murder? Does she think he's capable of that?

Ronan blinks first. "Why would I do something like that?"

"You said you saw him with your bracelet." It's what she's been thinking. She might as well say it.

"You think I killed your boyfriend over a bracelet?"

"I was there when the police found him," she says. It's close enough to the truth. "They also found a button, Ronan. A military button."

"So?"

"I recognized it. It's from your jacket. The one you were wearing that night."

There is no emotion at all on his face now.

"There are a lot of buttons like that around."

She stares at him. He stares at her. Why did she come here? What did she think was going to happen? What did she think she would accomplish?

"I just thought I'd let you know," she says finally. "They found the button. They asked Derek's mom about it. If they ask around enough, they'll find out that I used to go out with you and they might want to talk to you."

"Why?" As if he can't possibly imagine.

"They might think you have something against Derek."

He's quiet for a moment, thinking this over. "You mean," he says at last, "they might think I was jealous that you were seeing him instead of me and might think I killed him?" She doesn't answer. "Interesting theory. Except for one thing. I'm the one who broke up with you. You remember that, right? So why would I be jealous?"

Jesus, he's such an asshole sometimes. He just can't miss a chance to rub it in. She turns to go. As she takes the first step away from him, she realizes she's waiting for him to grab her arm and hold her back. Or tell her to wait. But all she hears is the scraping of the snow shovel against the surface of the ice as he goes back to clearing a skating rink.

Thirteen

When Jordie gets home, her parents and Carly are back from the funeral. As she heads upstairs, she hears voices coming from her sister's room.

"Carly?"

The voices stop.

"Carly, who are you talking to?"

"No one."

Right. Like Jordie is so stupid she can't distinguish two separate voices.

"I heard someone, Carly."

"It's the radio."

Uh-huh. Jordie wraps her hand around Carly's door-knob, twists and pushes the door. Carly, knowing her sister only too well, has positioned herself in front of the door, and it doesn't give.

"Let me in, Carly," Jordie says, suspicious now. More than suspicious—convinced that something is up and that she knows exactly what it is.

"No. It's my room, and you can't come in unless I invite you."

Jordie pushes again.

Carly screams for their mom, who is downstairs in the kitchen, contemplating how to use the last of the Christmas turkey.

"What is going on up there?" Mrs. Cross shouts.

"Jordie's trying to get into my room, and I don't want her to," Carly shrieks.

An exasperated-sounding Mrs. Cross tells Jordie she should know better and that if Carly and Tasha want private time, then Jordie has no choice but to respect that. "Do you understand me, Jordie?"

Jordie calls back that she does. Then she leans in close to the door, and in a stage whisper that Carly can hear but her mother can't, she says, "Maybe I should tell Mom about you-know-what. Then you can have a month of private time—without Tasha."

There is silence. The door opens. Carly stares acidly at her sister. Behind her, cross-legged on the bed, is Tasha Nelson.

"Aren't you going to invite me in?" Jordie asks. "Or do you want to have this conversation downstairs, say, in the kitchen?"

Carly steps aside. Jordie enters the cluttered room. Carly swings the door shut.

"Hi, Tasha," Jordie says sweetly. "Did Carly ask you about my bracelet?"

"We were just talking about that," Carly says at the exact same time that Tasha says, "What bracelet?" Tasha sounds genuinely curious.

Jordie glowers at her sister's reddening face. "You stole from me and then you *lied* to me? You said you texted her, Carly."

"I did text her."

"What bracelet?" Tasha asks again.

Jordie turns to her. "Carly told me she sold you a bracelet."

"Oh," Tasha says. "Yeah. But that was, like, a month ago. At least."

"Did she tell you where she got it?" Jordie asks.

"Sure."

Jordie glances at her sister, who is frantically shaking her head.

"Knock it off, Carly," Jordie says. Back to Tasha. "What did she tell you?"

"That she bought it and then decided she didn't like it, but she got it on sale, so she asked me if I wanted to buy it. It was cute, so I said yes."

"Well, she didn't buy it on sale. She stole it from me. And I want it back."

Tasha looks surprised, and again, the surprise appears genuine. Clearly, Carly lied about the bracelet's provenance. Surprise gives way to an agonized expression.

"I can't give it back," Tasha says.

"Why not?"

"Because *I* sold it to someone else."

Carly groans.

"I got a great price for it," Tasha says brightly. Almost instantly, regret flashes in her eyes. "But I spent it all. On Christmas presents."

"Who did you sell it to?"

Tasha exchanges glances with Carly. "Adam Noyes."

"Adam Noyes?" Adam is in Jordie's class. He's a jock, not a jewelry connoisseur. "How did that happen?"

"I was in the cafeteria asking around, and he liked the price." Here she glances at Carly. "What an idiot. You won't believe how much he paid for it."

"It's sterling silver," Jordie says. "And an antique. A genuine antique."

Carly's face falls. "You mean I could have got more for it?"

"Does he still have it?" Jordie demands.

"I don't know. I guess so. Unless he gave it to someone, you know, as a Christmas present."

"Who would he give it to?" Carly says. "He and Nicki broke up three weeks ago."

"Maybe he gave it to her before they broke up," Tasha says. "Or maybe he gave it to someone else as a Christmas present. Maybe his mom."

"You better hope not," Jordie says, angry at Tasha even though, strictly speaking, she acted in good faith. "I want it back."

"So go ask him," Carly says. Under her breath she mutters, "And good luck with that."

Jordie hears her and turns on her. She grabs Carly's wrist and twists it hard until Carly lets out a yowl. Their mother's muffled voice comes from below. "What's going on up there?" Jordie twists Carly's wrist again until Carly shouts out, "Nothing. We're just fooling around!"

Jordie maintains her grip on her sister's wrist. "I should make you go and ask him."

Carly waits. She has heard the magic word—*should*—and knows better than to say anything.

Jordie releases her with a shove, sending Carly careening back against her dresser. She storms out of the room. She doesn't hear the huge sigh of relief that escapes her sister.

>> >> >>

"Where are you going now?" Jordie's mother asks. "You just got in."

"I have to run an errand." Jordie is out the door before her mother can say another word. She hikes the seven blocks to the new subdivision filled with almost identical large houses on almost identical postage-stamp-sized pieces of land that are surrounded by almost identical privacy fences. The house she wants is in the middle of the block. She hurries up the neatly shoveled front walk and rings the bell.

Jordie has never met Mr. or Mrs. Noyes, but there they are, both at the door, Mr. Noyes doing the actual opening while Mrs. Noyes hovers behind him, holding a cardboard box in her arms labeled *Christmas ornaments*.

"I was wondering if Adam is here," Jordie says. When the two adults look quizzically at her, she hastily introduces herself, adding, "Adam is in some of my classes."

Mrs. Noyes smiles so broadly that Jordie is afraid she has misunderstood. Maybe she thinks Jordie is Adam's new girlfriend.

"Is he here?" Jordie prompts.

"He is indeed," Mr. Noyes says. "He's in the basement. You can go down if you want."

"Oh." She doesn't want to go down to the basement. She doesn't even want to go into the house. She doesn't know Adam well. It's true he is in two of her classes, but he is new to her school—new to town, in fact—and she can't recall ever having spoken to him. "Well, I have my boots on and—"

"Pull them off," Mr. Noyes says jovially, moving aside so that she can step onto a generous boot mat inside the door.

Jordie pulls off her boots. She glances around.

"First door on the right," Mr. Noyes says, indicating a hallway with an enthusiastic sweep of one arm.

Jordie pads down the hall in stocking feet. She opens the door. The stairs are wooden. The basement is unfinished. She creeps down the stairs and finds Adam in one corner, washing what turns out to be a Christmas-tree stand in a utility sink.

"Adam?"

He jumps and spins around. "You startled me." Then he squints at her, seemingly at a loss.

"I'm Jordie." He should know that, but maybe he doesn't. Maybe he's never even noticed her. "I'm in your—"

"Math and English classes," he finishes. "I know."

"I'm sorry to barge in on you, but your dad said you were down here."

"Which I am."

He turns off the tap and begins to dry the Christmas-tree stand with a rag. "My mom is kind of anal. Everything has to gleam all the time, even if she isn't going to see it again for a whole year." He drops the stand into a plastic bag, which he closes with a twist tie. Then he waits patiently for her to speak.

"This is kind of awkward," she says.

"I don't bite."

"It's about a bracelet you bought from my sister's friend Tasha."

He smiles right away. "Sterling silver. Early Victorian." She is stunned.

He laughs. "I showed it to my mom. She's the one who recognized it for what it was."

Was? That doesn't sound good.

Then he says, "Do you like it?"

"Excuse me?"

His eyes flit to her wrist. He frowns and shifts awkwardly. "I'm sorry," he says. "I thought…well, I guess I assumed…" His voice peters out.

"Do you have the bracelet, Adam?"

"Maugham has it."

"Mom? You gave it to your mom?"

"Not my mom. Derek Maugham."

"What?" She can't believe what she's hearing.

"I bought the bracelet from that kid, Tasha. She was trying to unload it. She had no idea how valuable it was." Like he got the better of her.

"You didn't either, from what you just said," Jordie points out.

"True. But I got it cheap. Then Maugham tells me he's looking for something special for his girl." Here he frowns. "I thought that was you."

"It is."

"So, what, he didn't give it to you yet?"

"It was supposed to be an anniversary present. He was going to give it to me on New Year's Eve. And then…" Her voice trails off.

"Yeah, I heard," Adam says. "They have any idea who did it?"

Jordie shakes her head. "Adam, are you telling me you sold the bracelet to Derek? I mean, he paid you and you handed it over to him?"

He nods. "If he didn't give it to you yet, it's probably at his house."

He's right. Derek must have gone to get it, just like he said he would. But someone killed him before he made it home. Or he did get home and got it, and someone killed him on the way back to her house. She's not sure which. So the bracelet must be either in his room among his things or on him—assuming, that is, that it wasn't stolen by whoever killed him. She wonders for the first time if anything *was* stolen—his watch, maybe, or his wallet.

"I'm really sorry about what happened to him," Adam says. "I never knew anyone who was killed. Murdered, I mean."

Jordie thanks him and heads back up the stairs. If Derek had the bracelet, and if it wasn't stolen, then the police must have found it on him. Do they still have it? Or have they returned it to his parents? It's a murder case, so she's not sure how long the police hang on to things.

Ronan Barthe pushes the snow shovel up and back across the ice. Up and back. Up and back. After each length, he turns to look at Jordie, who is retreating across the ice. The very last time he looks, she is gone. She has rounded the point and is back where the big houses are. She'll go up the stairs that allow for public access to the lakefront.

Ronan shoulders the shovel and skates back to the shore on his side of the point. He's left his boots there, on top of a snow-covered rock. He sweeps some snow aside and plunks himself down to unlace his skates. He pulls on his boots, ties the laces of his skates together and slings the skates over his shoulder before grabbing the snow shovel and climbing up to the road.

He walks home. It takes nearly twenty minutes.

"Mom?" he calls after he's stamped the snow off his boots on the rubber mat inside the front door.

He gets no answer. She's probably sleeping.

He hangs his skates on a hook, stands the snow shovel in the corner of the little landing and opens the door to the kitchen. He shrugs out of his jacket as he heads up the stairs. A peek into his mother's bedroom confirms that she is asleep. He stands in the door for a few seconds, watching for the rise and fall of her chest. Funny, he thinks, how he's got into the habit of doing that. Funny, too, in a worrisome way, that before he finally registers the almost imperceptible movement, he is gripped by panic, because what will he do if she isn't breathing? It's the one thing he doesn't want to think about and the one thing he knows is coming at him faster than he would like to believe.

He tiptoes across the room to a cupboard under the window and opens it. There's a small basket inside. He carries it with him out of the room.

Moments later, he is perched on his bed, his army-surplus jacket in hand, sorting through the basket—his mother's sewing basket—for some navy-blue thread.

There isn't any.

Black will have to do.

He threads a needle and sticks it into his bedspread while he pulls out a small pair of scissors. He turns his jacket inside out, locates the spare button that is sewn onto an inside seam and cuts it loose. With needle and thread, he sews the spare button onto the front of his jacket to replace the one that was ripped off. If anyone asks, and he doubts they will unless Jordie decides to say something to the cops, he will say that he lost a button ages ago and sewed it back on then. Who can say different?

Problem solved.

Fourteen

Jordie is barely listening that night as her mother makes table talk about the funeral. She's trying to figure out how she's going to do what she desperately needs to do. She's nervous about it. The truth is, she hasn't known anyone her age who died. She's never had to deal with people she knows, adult people, who are grieving. She's not sure she'll have any idea what to say. And what if she says the *wrong* thing? God, that would be terrible. She might make things worse.

"...set aside to look after her," her mother is saying.

"Well, he won't have to worry about that now," Mr. Cross says. "In fact, if I were him—"

"Can I make muffins after supper?" Jordie asks.

"Excuse me, I'm sure," Mr. Cross says.

"Your father was talking, Jordana," her mother says.

"Sorry, Dad. Can I, Mom? I want to take them over to Derek's parents. I mean, it's the least I can do."

"It's a lovely idea," Mrs. Cross says. She squeezes Jordie's hand. "I'm sure they'll have people dropping by, and I'm sure Marsha won't feel like baking."

"Hel-*lo*?" Mr. Cross says. "Does anyone care what I was saying?"

His wife smiles sweetly at him, but before she can answer, Carly cuts in.

"You were going to say that if you were him, you'd take the money from the sale of the old homestead, retire and buy a place down in Mexico or somewhere where a person can live like a king and never have to shovel snow or even look at it again." She grins. "Right, Dad?"

Both her parents are staring at her. Mr. Cross's mouth hangs open.

"I listened to every word you said," Carly crows. "So I was wondering, Dad—"

"Aha!" he says. "Now we get down to it."

Carly's smile is as sweet as her mother's. "Since I always pay attention to you, Daddy—"

"*Daddy*?" Jordie knows what's coming next. So does her father. He crosses his arms over his chest and leans back in his chair to wait.

"I was wondering if you could drive Tasha and me to Minton after supper to see a movie."

"Aha!" Mr. Cross says again.

"What will your father do while you two are at the movies?" Mrs. Cross asks. "It's an hour's drive each way. He won't be able to come home."

"I'll go to the movie with my daughter and her friend," Mr. Cross announces.

Carly blanches. "No way, Dad!"

Up go her father's eyebrows. "No way? You want me to do you this huge favour, but you don't welcome my presence?"

"I bet John Rocher is going to be there," Jordie says.

Carly scowls at her.

"Ah," says Mr. Cross. "Is this true, darling daughter?"

"Please, Daddy? We really want to go, and you're the only person who can drive us."

Her father presses a finger to his lips and looks up thoughtfully. "If I remember correctly, there's a bus that goes to Minton."

Carly howls. Jordie thinks about muffins. She can take them over and tell the Maughams how sorry she is and how awful it must be for them because it's awful for her and she's only Derek's girlfriend. In fact, she hates to ask, but...

Twenty minutes later, Carly and her father are leaving the house, Jordie is clearing the table, and her mother is looking for her famous graham-chocolate-chip muffin recipe.

It's colder than ever the next morning, with another few inches of snow on the ground. Jordie has to plod through it, lifting her legs higher than usual and, consequently, tiring faster, especially when she slogs up the hill to the Maughams' house. She carries a basket of muffins she and her mother made and a card she herself picked out and wrote in, which she hopes Mrs. Maugham will read only after Jordie leaves because for sure it will make her cry, and Jordie doesn't want to see that. She's nervous and keeps going over the approach she has worked out. But it doesn't sound right. It sounds phony, prying, as if she is more interested in herself than in how Derek's parents are feeling. She tries to revise it as she climbs the hill, panting and sweating into her clean T-shirt.

Mr. Maugham answers the doorbell. He smiles when he greets her, but she can tell from the gray skin under his eyes and the redness in their rims that he has been having trouble sleeping.

"My mom and I made these," Jordie says, holding out the basket of muffins.

"Come in," Mr. Maugham says. "Marsha isn't here. She's taken some clothes to the funeral home." He almost chokes on the words. His eyes are so sad that Jordie has to fight the urge to bolt. But he rallies and smiles at her. It's such a brilliant smile, so warm, so wistful, and she realizes that she is the closest thing they have to Derek now, that she represents him at his most recent, his most vital, his happiest—at least, that's what Mrs. Maugham has said to her constantly over the past couple of months: *I've never seen Derek happier than he is now; you're good for him, Jordie.*

She steps into the foyer. From there she can see into the kitchen, where cake tins and Tupperware containers and boxed sweets cover the table.

"You should see the fridge," Mr. Maugham says, following her gaze. "We have enough casseroles to last clear through to spring. I guess I should put some of them in the freezer..." His voice trails off.

"I can do that for you, Mr. Maugham," Jordie says, happy to have something to do to allow her to ease into the heavy atmosphere of the house. She pulls off her boots and coat and goes through to the kitchen.

The fridge shelves are stacked with glass and aluminum casserole pans, some covered in foil, some in plastic wrap. As Jordie carries them to the freezer in the mudroom at the back of the house, she notices that each is labeled on the bottom with the name of the woman who prepared and delivered it. She makes a note to herself to see that they are returned. She is sure Mrs. Maugham will not want to do it, not if it leaves her open to talk about Derek, to memories and to tears.

When she finishes, Mr. Maugham thanks her and presents her with a mug of tea.

"How are you holding up, Mr. Maugham?" Jordie asks.

He squeezes her hand. "About as well as you, I guess."

She doubts that. "And Mrs. Maugham?"

To her astonishment, his eyes grow instantly moist. He lifts his own mug of tea and turns away from her, seemingly so that he can look out the window.

"Mr. Maugham?"

He keeps his gaze steady on the window.

"She's doing her best. We're all doing our best."

Jordie wishes now that she hadn't come. The poor man is utterly crushed. Derek was his only son. Their only child. She sips the tea she doesn't even want.

"Did they—" She breaks off. How can she ask? But how can she not? "Mr. Maugham, I was wondering if they...if the police...if they gave you back Derek's belongings."

"His belongings?"

"What he had with him...at the time." God, this saying things without saying them is hard. She almost hates herself for even bothering the poor man.

Mr. Maugham sets down his cup and leans against the counter, his hands gripping its edges.

"I didn't want her to have to see him, not like that. I thought it would be easier if she remembered him the way he was, not the way he ended up. But she insisted. She may not look it, but she's stubborn. She said she had to see. His head—" He stifles a sob. Jordie waits. This is a mistake, she tells herself. But she can't leave him now, not after she's already reopened the wound. "They kept his clothes. They said they needed those. They kept his backpack too. They asked us if anything was missing, like maybe they thought someone had robbed him and he fought back, and that's why he was killed."

She waits for what she hopes is a respectful interval before she asks, "Was anything taken?"

"I don't think so. His wallet was there. His Christmas money was in it, and his debit card and credit card. He still had on his watch, not that it's worth much, and his phone. He's not one of those flashy kids. You know that. He doesn't carry around a lot of stuff. So whatever it was, now they think it wasn't robbery. It was something else."

"Did they give you back everything?"

Mr. Maugham nods. "There are pictures on the phone—quite a few of you and him together. His mother insisted on keeping that. She's been scrolling through them."

"I have a bunch of pictures on my phone too," Jordie says, feeling good for the first time since she arrived. "I can print them out for you if you want. Or email them to you. Or both."

Mr. Maugham's eyes get waterier. "That would be nice." He stares past Jordie, out the kitchen window. Jordie turns and looks too, and realizes that from where he is standing, he can see out over the tops of the trees below, down to where she found Derek's scarf, down to where he drew the last breath of his life. "I just don't understand who would do this to him," Mr. Maugham says. "He was a good kid. He didn't have any enemies that I know of. Did he, Jordie?"

Jordie meets Mr. Maugham's eyes. He is all but pleading for an answer.

"Everybody liked Derek," she says.

Slam! Mr. Maugham's fist, balled tight, comes down hard on the countertop, making Jordie jump.

"Clearly, everyone didn't." There is fire in his eyes. "Someone killed him. Someone killed my son. The police say he was hit on the head several times. The back of his head—" He breaks off, biting his lips, pressing them tightly together, trying, Jordie realizes, not to break down in front of her.

"Maybe the police are wrong," Jordie says. "Maybe it was meant to be a robbery, but something happened, something went wrong."

"I wish that was true," Mr. Maugham says. "It would be easier for his mother to think that some drug addict or crazy person tried to kill him for the few dollars in his wallet or for his cell phone than that someone did it out of hate or, I don't know, for no reason at all."

Jordie guesses it would be easier for Mr. Maugham too.

"I'm sure the police will find the person," she says, wondering if her confidence is warranted. She can't remember the last time there was a murder in town. She has no idea how many homicide investigations the local police have handled.

Mr. Maugham's gaze slips back to the kitchen window.

"Mr. Maugham, I was wondering…" Wondering what? She's pretty sure that if the police had found what she's looking for, Derek's father would have said so. So either whoever killed him took it, or…"Would it be okay if I saw Derek's room?"

"His room?" Mr. Maugham doesn't seem to understand.

"I was hoping—I would never take anything without your permission. Never. But I was hoping there might be something that Derek and I shared, something I could have, you know, to remember him by."

Mr. Maugham's face softens. A tear trickles down one cheek. "Of course."

"If there is anything, I'll show you first. I would never take anything without your okay." She feels she can't say this often enough.

"It's fine, Jordie. Go ahead."

Jordie leaves the rest of her tea on the kitchen table and starts up the carpeted stairs to the second floor. Derek's room is at the back of the house. The door is closed. She pushes it open. It looks exactly the way it looked the last time she saw it. It's always neat, but she knows that isn't because of Derek. It's Mrs. Maugham, not Derek, who changes the sheets, vacuums the floor, scrubs the sink and the toilet in his bathroom. It's Mrs. Maugham who sets his books and magazines neatly in their places, who dusts his dresser top and his desk, who folds his laundry and puts it away in his drawers.

Jordie steps across the threshold and looks around. Bed, bedside table, highboy dresser, mirror, desk, computer, beanbag chair, basketball hoop and Nerf basketball, bookshelves, stacks of hockey magazines, hockey posters on the wall, four or five hockey sticks leaning in one corner, hockey jersey framed on the wall. She can't remember whose it is. Not Gretzky's—ninety-nine is the only hockey number she knows, thanks to her dad, and this one isn't ninety-nine.

She creeps to the bedside table. Besides the lamp on it, there's a science fiction novel with a bookmark in it from where Derek left off reading, a small framed picture of Derek and Jordie together at the mall, smiling at each other, and a Bart Simpson clock—not the digital kind, but the kind with an hour hand and a second hand, and it's showing the wrong time. The glass over the clock face is broken, and when Jordie picks up the clock to wind it, something inside rattles. The clock is broken. She sets it down and slides open the bedside table's lone drawer. Keys, an old combination lock, a bunch of matchbox cars with chips of paint missing, a Sesame Street Cookie Counter, which makes her smile, a heap of pennies—but not what she is looking for. She slides the drawer back in. From there it's to the desk, then the highboy and finally the top shelf of his closet, where he has stacks of boxes that turn out to contain hockey cards (five boxes full) and shoes (four boxes). She keeps glancing at the door as she searches, worried that Mr. Maugham will show up and wonder what she's doing. But if it's here, she can't find it. Does that mean he had it with him when he—when he died?

Did whoever killed him take it? Or do the cops have it? Is there some way she can find out?

She is about to leave when she recalls what she told Mr. Maugham. She goes to his closet and pulls out one of Derek's old hockey sweaters. She holds it to her nose and inhales. It smells like Derek. She's still holding it to her face when a voice behind her says, "What do you think you're doing?"

Jordie whirls around.

"Mrs. Maugham, I thought—"

"You thought what?" There is none of the kindness, none of the warmth, in her eyes that Jordie saw in her husband's. Mrs. Maugham's voice is sharp. She glowers at Jordie. She is angry with her, but Jordie doesn't know why.

"Mr. Maugham said you were out. He said it was okay if I—"

"He told me what he said. And he's wrong. I don't want you touching Derek's things." She stares at the sweater Jordie is holding and, before Jordie can do anything, snatches it out of Jordie's hands.

"I'm sorry, I—"

"How did you know where he was?" Mrs. Maugham demands.

"What?"

"Derek. You came up here and told us that he'd come home that night. You didn't say why. And the next thing I know, you're out behind the house and the police are here, looking where you told them to look. There were search parties out looking for Derek, but you're the one who finds him. *You*. What happened that night? What did you do to my Derek?"

Jordie is horrified by the turn the conversation has taken. "I didn't do anything. I was home all night."

"Something happened." Mrs. Maugham clutches the sweater. "He was supposed to stay with you. He was supposed to be safe there. But he didn't stay. He left. Why?"

"I told you. We had a little argument—"

"Did he break up with you? Is that it? Did he break up with you and leave, and you followed him and... and..." Her eyes go to the bedside table. She reaches for something. The clock. "Did you do this?" she demands, holding it up for Jordie to see. "Did you break this?"

"No," Jordie says. "It was like that."

Mrs. Maugham tries to wind the clock—to no avail. Tears start to flow down her cheeks.

"I don't want you touching his things. Not after what you did."

After what I *did?*

"I would never hurt Derek." It's the absolute truth. Jordie has never hurt anyone, not physically anyway. "Never. I *liked* Derek."

"*Liked*? You *liked* him? All he ever did was talk about you. He told anyone who would listen that he loved you, and you *liked* him? Get out." Mrs. Maugham is trembling with rage. "Get out of my house and don't ever come back. If it wasn't for you, Derek would still be alive."

"But Mrs. Maugham—"

"Get out! Get out!" She's shrieking the words at Jordie now, and when Jordie shrinks past her and starts down the stairs, Mrs. Maugham follows her, still screaming.

Mr. Maugham is at the bottom of the stairs, staring up at his wife and at Jordie.

"Marsha, what's wrong?"

"She's responsible. She drove our son out of her house that night. If he'd stayed put, he'd still be alive!"

Mr. Maugham whispers an apology as Jordie passes him.

"Don't you dare apologize to her!" Mrs. Maugham shrieks. "She knows more than she's letting on. I'm going to talk to the police about you. I'm going to tell them what you did!"

Jordie pulls her boots on as fast as her trembling hands will allow. She scrambles out the door and runs around the side of the house. She doesn't look back until she is halfway down to the rail trail. When she does, she sees Mrs. Maugham framed in the kitchen window, a telephone pressed against her ear.

Carly is sitting halfway down the stairs the next morning at ten thirty when Jordie finally gets out of bed. Jordie can't believe she's slept so late.

"What's—"

Carly raises a finger to her lips to silence her. "The cops are here," she whispers.

"What for?"

"They're asking Mom and Dad about Derek and you."

Jordie sinks down beside her sister. "What about me?"

But Carly is batting the air to silence her again. Too late. The voices have stopped. Jordie hears footsteps on the hardwood.

"Carly!" It's their father. "Carly, get down here."

Carly runs down the stairs.

"Lieutenant Diehl wants to ask you some questions," Mr. Cross says. "You can talk to her in the living room, lieutenant."

Jordie stays where she is and listens to her father retreat to the kitchen. Lieutenant Diehl introduces himself. He uses a tone more appropriate for a kindergarten kid than for a fourteen-year-old like Carly, but Carly doesn't bristle the way she does when anyone else talks down to her. As far as Jordie knows, she has never been questioned by a cop before.

"Do you want one of your parents here while we talk?" Diehl asks.

"Are you going to arrest me for something?" Carly does not sound remotely intimidated.

"No. I just want to ask you a few questions about Derek Maugham. You know what happened, don't you?"

"Someone killed him."

"That's right. Did you know him very well?"

"I guess. He was my sister's boyfriend."

"I understand he was here the weekend before he died."

"Yeah. His folks went out of town, but he couldn't tear himself away from Jordie—don't ask me why. So he stayed here. My parents are practically more in love with him than she is, if she's even in love with him anymore."

Jeez, why did she say that?

"What do you mean, Carly? Did Derek and your sister have an argument?"

"No. Not that I know of anyway. What I mean is, my mom thinks he's the best thing ever, especially compared to Jordie's old boyfriend." Jordie could kill her sister about now. "I think my mom wishes she'd marry someone like Derek. She invites him over all the time. And he's always doing stuff that makes my dad think he's the greatest, especially, since, you know, he's got two daughters and doesn't have the son he always wanted. Derek helps him when he's playing Mr. Handyman or whatever." Carly is talking fast, which she only ever does when she's laying it on, trying to distract whoever she's talking to from the truth. But there's no way Diehl would know that.

"So they didn't have an argument?"

"Who?"

"Your sister and Derek."

Jordie thinks she catches a hint of irritation.

"Not that I know of."

"Were you here the whole weekend that Derek was here?"

"Sure. My best friend Tasha got to go to Florida with her parents. To Disney World. But my parents never want to do anything that fun. They make a big deal about Christmas. Mostly we sit around and get bored out of our skulls."

She's avoiding saying something, Jordie is sure of it. But what?

"And Derek? Was he here the whole time?"

"He and Jordie went to the mall one day. And I think they took a couple of walks. Why?"

"Did he ever leave the house without your sister?"

"He went out to shovel with my dad."

"Besides that, did he leave the house alone?"

"How would I know?" She's talking to him now the way she talks to their parents—without any reverence or respect.

"You didn't hear anything strange the night before he went missing, like maybe someone sneaking out of the house or into it?"

"No. Why? You think someone broke into our house?"

"You go to the same high school as your sister and Derek, correct?"

"Cor-*rect*." Now she's flat-out mocking him. Jordie wonders how he feels about that.

"The way I recall high school, someone sees something and it gets around school pretty fast."

"Probably way faster than you remember," Carly says, "what with cell phones and Facebook and Twitter and stuff."

"Was there anything going around about Derek and anyone else? Anyone he didn't get along with or someone who maybe had a grudge against him?"

Jordie holds her breath.

"You mean, besides Ronan?"

Jordie wants to strangle her sister.

"Ronan?" Diehl says.

"Jordie's old boyfriend."

"This Ronan—what's his last name?"

"Barthe. Ronan Barthe."

"He had a grudge against Derek?"

"Well, duh," Carly says. "Jordie broke up with him and started going with Derek."

"And he didn't take it well?"

"Would you?"

"Did he make trouble for Derek?"

"I heard he was really pissed at him."

"You heard? What specifically did you hear?"

"Just what I told you."

"Did you ever see the two of them together—Derek and Ronan? Did you ever see them fight or argue?"

"No. But I bet if you ask around, you'll find someone who did. Because I heard that Ronan was ready to punch Derek out—"

Jordie knows then that she has to do something. She screams.

She hears footsteps on the kitchen tile. The door opens and her father runs for the stairs. By the time he gets there, Jordie is on her feet, her head in her hands, and she is sobbing for all she's worth. She chances a peek through her fingers and sees Carly and her mom behind her dad. In the background is Diehl.

"I—I had a nightmare. It was about Derek."

Her mother nudges her father aside, comes up the stairs and wraps her arms around Jordie. Carly is frowning. Please, please, please, don't say another word, Jordie thinks.

Her dad turns to Diehl.

"We're going to have to continue this another time," he says.

Diehl's face is bland, unreadable, but he nods. "No problem. Maybe you could bring Carly by later in the day, or maybe tomorrow. It's not urgent."

Jordie's dad thanks him and shows him to the door. Jordie's mom guides her upstairs to her room. Carly follows.

"Keep your sister company," Mrs. Cross tells Carly. "I'll put the kettle on for tea."

"Great idea, Mom," Carly says. "There hasn't been a problem created that a cup of steaming tea can't solve."

If Celia hears the sarcasm in her younger daughter's voice, she gives no sign of it.

Carly plops down on the side of Jordie's bed. "Really? A nightmare? When you were already awake?" More sarcasm. Always more.

"I had to shut you up somehow."

"Shut me up? What did I say that was so bad?"

"Did you have to drag Ronan into this?"

"I was just answering questions," Carly says. "And anyway, since when do you care about Ronan? Last I heard, he was poison to you. And for all you know, he could have been the one to smash Derek's head in."

"He would never!"

Carly rears back. There is nothing fake or dramatic about the gesture. She is impressed by her sister's vehemence. "Mr. Devil Incarnate is now some kind of angel of sweetness and light?"

"He's not a murderer, and you know it."

"No, I don't." Carly is back to her unflustered self. "And I'm sure you don't want me to lie to the police, do you?"

"Why not? You lie to Mom and Dad all the time. You probably lie to me too." Jordie is furious.

"Okay, fine, so I won't say anything else about Ronan to the cops."

"Great." But Jordie knows it's already too late. She has no doubt that Diehl will follow up on what Carly has told him.

"But it's not going to make any difference."

"Because?"

"Because if the cops talk to anyone at school, they'll tell them that Ronan was pissed at Derek for"—air quotes come into play—"*stealing* you from him. And if they talk to Deedee, well, it'll probably be game over for him."

Deedee is one of Carly's massive circle of annoying ninth-
grade friends.

The stealing part, of course, isn't true. The breakup
was Ronan's call, but Jordie never told her sister that. She
never told anyone, but especially not Carly. The taunts
would only have caused more strife than usual: *You got
dumped by Ronan Barthe? What a loser—you, Jordie, not
him.* But what's this about Deedee?

"What do you mean? What does Deedee have to do
with anything?"

"She was the one who told me when it happened.
She was there."

"When what happened?"

"When Ronan was ready to pulverize Derek, which
he would have done if Mr. Merriwether hadn't come
along. Jeez, I don't get how a guy that big and that built—
he looks like he could knock the crap out of Tyson or
Holyfield or any of those guys—ends up with a name
like Carmine Merriwether. If names had anything to do
with the people who walked around with them, he'd be
named, I don't know, John Widowmaker or Jack Death.
He wouldn't have such a girly doofus name."

"Now, Carly, you know it isn't nice to make fun of
people's names." It's their mother, with a mug of steaming
tea and a plate of cookies, both of which she hands to
Jordie.

"Gee, Mom, you shouldn't have," Carly says, all
sarcastic again.

"You have a dishwasher to empty, young lady."

"It's Jordie's turn!"

"Scoot," says Mrs. Cross.

"Let her stay for a few minutes, Mom," Jordie says.

Of course, Carly jumps up off the bed, ready to leave now that she's been asked—well, sort of—to stay.

"Come on, Carly, stay. I'll empty the dishwasher for you. I promise."

"For real promise?"

"For real."

Carly sits down again. Mrs. Cross sighs.

"It's moments like these, rare as they are, that I cherish. You girls have no idea how much I wished I'd had a sister instead of four brothers." She kisses Carly on the top of her head. "Never mind. *I'll* empty the dishwasher."

"Thanks, Mom," Jordie says.

"Thanks, Mom," Carly mutters in irritation once her mother is out of earshot. "I totally don't get what you ever did to be treated like a princess around here, Little Miss Perfect. Jeez, if Mom only knew…"

"You were telling me about Ronan and Derek," Jordie says.

"And you were about to promise that you'd empty the dishwasher for the entire month of January."

"Now you're blackmailing me?"

"Don't be silly. You're *incentivizing* me."

Jordie rolls her eyes. "Okay. Whatever."

"You know what happens when you break a promise, right?"

"Just tell me about Derek and Ronan."

"Pass the cookies."

Jordie feels like throwing the plate at her. "Spill."

Carly takes a bite of a Santa sugar cookie. "Deedee says she was at her locker on the last day of school, and she heard a loud bang, like someone had slammed into a locker around the corner. So she went to take a look. Ronan had Derek up against a bank of lockers outside one of the chem labs, and he was telling him he wanted what was his."

"What did he mean?" Jordie asks, even though she knows what it was about because Derek told her.

"What do you think?" Carly can't keep the sarcasm from her voice. "You." She takes another bite of cookie. "Don't ask me why though."

It's clear that neither Carly nor Deedee knows about the bracelet.

"Then what happened?"

"According to Deedee, Derek said no. So Ronan grabbed him by the shoulders and yanked him forward and slammed him against the lockers again. Hard. Deedee said Derek's head hit pretty hard. Then she said it looked like Ronan was going to punch him. She said he had this totally homicidal look in his eyes."

Jordie wonders if Deedee's telling of the tale was as dramatic as Carly's.

"Deedee said she was ready to call 9-1-1. Then Mr. Merriwether came out of the bathroom and that was the end of that."

"He broke it up?"

"More like he sized up the situation and asked them if there was a problem. Deedee said Ronan backed off right away, and Derek said no, there was no problem. Ronan glowered at him and then he just walked away."

"Do you know if Deedee told anyone besides you about what she saw?"

Carly shrugs. "Maybe. I dunno. Maybe she only told me because you used to go out with Ronan."

"Can you find out?"

"Find out what?"

"If she told anyone. And if she did, who she told."

"What if she did?"

"I want to talk to her. In fact, is she around? Because if she is, let's go and see her now."

Carly's eyes narrow. She regards her sister with undisguised suspicion.

"Why? What are you planning to do?"

"I just want to talk to her, that's all." Jordie stands up suddenly. "Text her now. See if she's around."

"What are you up to?" Carly asks, even more suspicious now. "You're going to ask her to lie to the police, aren't you?"

Jordie feels her cheeks flush. "I just want to talk to her, Carly."

"What if the cops ask me who told me that story about Ronan and Derek?"

"You tell them you don't remember."

"Aha!" Carly leaps to her feet. "I was right. You want me to lie to the police. Why? Are you protecting Ronan? Why would you even do that? You haven't talked to him in months."

Jordie turns away—but too late.

"You *have* talked to him! You have, haven't you?" Carly circles her sister to get a good look at her face. "Are you and Ronan back together? Is that it?"

"No."

"Did Ronan kill Derek?"

"Of course not! How can you say such a thing?"

"But you're afraid the police will think he did, aren't you? That's why you want to know if Deedee told anyone else what she saw. Isn't it?"

"Do you want me to tell Mom you stole my bracelet? *And* sold it?"

"Do you want *me* to tell Mom that your ex-boyfriend killed your current boyfriend—and that you're trying to cover it up?"

"That's not true!"

"Mom!"

Jordie clamps a hand over her sister's mouth. "Shut up, Carly, or you'll regret it."

"What's going on up there?" Mrs. Cross calls from the bottom of the stairs.

"Nothing," Jordie calls back.

There is a moment of silence, then: "Carly? Carly, what's going on?"

Jordie keeps her hand firmly in place. "Tell her it's nothing, Carly."

Carly squirms. Her voice is muffled, but Jordie is pretty sure she says, "What's in it for me?"

"If you promise you won't say anything about what you told me until I say you can, I'll give you anything you want."

Carly's greedy eyes get enormous. She nods.

Jordie releases her hand.

"Nothing's going on, Mom," Carly shouts down to her mother. "Except that Jordie's being the usual big-sister pain in the—"

"Watch your language, young lady," Mrs. Cross warns.

The two girls wait. Their mother doesn't come upstairs. Nor does she say anything else. Finally Jordie says, "Text Deedee and see if she's home."

"I have to get my phone."

Jordie nods. Carly disappears. When she comes back into Jordie's room, she is holding her phone and texting with her thumbs. A few seconds after she stops, the phone buzzes.

"She's home," Carly announces.

"We're going over."

"Wait a minute. You said if I help you with this, you'll give me whatever I want."

Jordie sighs. She knows she is going to regret it. "And that would be?"

"You do my kitchen chores for the whole year."

"What? You little mercenary! I didn't mean I'd turn myself into a galley slave for you."

"You said anything. If you don't want to stick to the deal we made, that's okay by me. But it means I don't stick to my end either."

Jordie wants to scream. But she needs to keep everything quiet—if she can—until she figures out what's going on. After that, she'll find a way to renegotiate.

"Okay," she says.

"I want it in writing."

"Oh for god's sake!"

"In writing or it doesn't happen."

Jordie knows her sister has her over a barrel, and she hates it. But she grabs a piece of paper and a pen from her desk and writes what Carly dictates. She dates the page, signs it and thrusts it into her sister's hands. Carly beams as she rereads it.

"Suitable for framing," she murmurs.

Jordie grabs her sister by the arm and shoves her out of the room. "I'll meet you downstairs."

As she hurriedly dresses, Jordie prays that Deedee has kept quiet about this one thing. Because there is no way Jordie will entertain the notion that Ronan killed Derek, although she isn't so sure what other people will think.

Fifteen

Deirdre "Deedee" Sullivan lives in one of the two subdivisions built on former farms on what used to be the outskirts of town. The house is three times bigger than Jordie and Carly's house, but, as Mrs. Cross crows triumphantly, it sits on about half the amount of land and is so close to its neighbors that "you can look out of your dining room window and see what they're having for supper next door."

Jordie loves these big houses with their formal living rooms and dining rooms, and their huge eat-in kitchens and just-as-huge family rooms, not to mention their large bedrooms and seemingly infinite number of bathrooms. Jordie's life would be blessed if she didn't have to share a bathroom with her sister.

Deedee is delighted to see Carly but puzzled by Jordie's presence.

"She wants to talk to you," Carly explains with a complete absence of enthusiasm. "Can we come in?"

"I guess." Deedee frowns as she regards Jordie. "Sorry about your boyfriend," she says finally. "I guess you must be...devastated?" She speaks the last word as a question, as if she isn't entirely sure she has used the right word.

Jordie mumbles a thank-you.

Deedee waits as the two girls shed their boots and coats. She leads them up the staircase that cuts through the two-story atrium foyer. Deedee's room, large and sunny yellow, is at the back of the house, overlooking a fenced-in, covered-for-winter swimming pool. Deedee shuts the door and flops down on her bed.

"So, what's up?"

Carly turns to Jordie and, with a wave of her arm, invites her to take center stage.

Jordie perches on the edge of Deedee's desk chair.

"This is kind of about Derek," she says. She peers at her sister's friend. Deedee is one of those tiny girls—petite, perfectly proportioned and with delicate features and light honey-blond hair; she reminds Jordie of a porcelain figurine. She knows nothing about Deedee. Will raising the subject send her into the arms of the police with something valuable to relate, something that might break open a murder investigation? Or can this girl be trusted, on the strength of whatever her relationship is to

Carly, to keep her mouth shut? Is Jordie about to make things better—or worse?

Deedee is watching her. So is Carly. Carly rolls her eyes.

"Remember that thing you saw between Derek and Ronan?" Carly asks, brisk and businesslike.

Deedee's barely-there blond eyebrows knit together and she appears to search her memory.

"You know, the time when you saw them and it looked like Ronan was going to punch Derek out?" Carly prods, exasperated.

Deedee's face brightens. "Oh, yeah." She smiles almost beatifically, which makes Jordie wonder if there's something wrong with her. "I don't care what everyone says." Her voice is as dreamy as her expression. "I think Ronan is superhot."

Carly rolls her eyes again. "You told me about what you saw, remember?"

"Sure."

"Did you tell anyone else?"

Deedee's cornflower-blue eyes widen a fraction. "Did I tell anyone else?"

"That's the question on the table," Carly says, stunning her sister with her superior attitude. For the first time ever, Jordie wonders what role her sister plays in her coterie of friends. Is she the queen bee? Or does she just act like the queen bee with the girls whom she perceives as lower on the social order than herself? Whichever it is, Deedee appears to take no offense.

"I don't think so," Deedee says finally. "Why?"

"But you told Carly," Jordie says, jumping in before Carly can say anything. "Why did you tell her?"

Deedee has to think about this. "Well, I told her because I thought she would be interested, you know, because you used to go out with Ronan and then you were going out with..." She hesitates. "You know."

"Derek." Jordie says it to prove that mentioning his name won't reduce her to tears.

Deedee nods.

"But you didn't tell anyone else?" Jordie asks.

Deedee shakes her head.

"Are you sure, Deedee?" Carly demands.

Where does she get off talking to her friends in that tone of voice?

"I'm sure," Deedee says in a small voice. "Why? Should I have?"

Carly opens her mouth to speak. Jordie silences her with a cutting glance.

"No, you shouldn't have," Jordie says. "If you ask me, people talk too much about things they know nothing about. Not that you would ever do that, Deedee," she adds quickly. "You seem like the kind of person who doesn't go around spreading rumors."

Deedee's eyes widen, and she sits a little taller. "I try not to."

"And that's good," Jordie says. "Somebody killed Derek." Deedee winces, and Jordie does her best to look stricken as she mentions his name. "I don't know who did it. But I would hate for someone who had nothing to do with it to get blamed, all on account of some rumor or something that someone saw without knowing the whole story. You know what I mean, right, Deedee?"

"You want me not to say anything about what I saw?" Her eyebrows knit together again. She looks as confused as she sounds.

"I sure don't want you to spread rumors about anyone. You don't want to do that, do you, Deedee? I mean, what if Carly got killed and then someone told the police they'd seen the two of you fighting, and on the basis of that the police decided you killed her, even though you had nothing to do with it? Once the police make up their minds about something, it's next to impossible for them to change it. I know. I did a project last year on wrongful convictions. You don't want to be responsible for anything like that, do you, Deedee?"

Deedee shakes her head slowly. "I like Ronan," she says. "He seems so lonely and so unhappy, you know?"

Jordie stares at the girl, surprised. Ronan is often alone, that's for sure. He doesn't smile much. But lonely and unhappy? Is he really, or is that simply the prism through which this naïve little porcelain doll sees him?

"I would never want anyone to think that I think he could do something evil." Deedee looks directly at Jordie. "I won't say anything if you don't want me to."

"That's great, Deedee."

"Unless the police ask me," Deedee adds.

What? "Why would the police ask *you* about Derek and Ronan?" Jordie asks.

"I'm just saying. I would never lie to the police. Lying is wrong. It's a sin. If the police ask me if I ever saw Derek and Ronan fighting, I would have to tell them the truth."

Jordie glances at Carly. Carly gestures with a quick nod of the head toward Deedee's bedside table, where Jordie sees a Bible and a book about Christian morality.

"Of course you would have to tell the truth," Jordie says. She can't imagine a police officer approaching Deedee and asking her flat-out if she's ever witnessed an altercation or any other problem between the two boys. Deedee is two years younger than Jordie. To the best of Jordie's knowledge, Deedee has never spoken to either boy. "But you also don't want to spread rumors that could hurt someone badly."

Deedee nods solemnly. "I won't say anything unless I have to. I feel sorry for Ronan. I think he needs a friend."

Jordie thanks her. Carly stands up.

"See you at school," Carly says.

Deedee beams as if she has been specially chosen to be part of a queen's court.

"I thought she was your friend," Jordie says to her sister as they walk away from the house.

"Who told you that?"

Jordie has to think for a moment. She realizes it was an assumption.

"Her dad is one of those evangelical preachers. He has a show on cable TV. She's kind of weird. But she's in a bunch of my classes, and it's like she can't take a hint. She's always hanging around. She's as hard to shake as a leech. Everyone thinks she's nuts."

No wonder, Jordie thinks, that Deedee sees Ronan as lonely. She looks at him and thinks she is looking into a mirror.

"Do you think she'll stay quiet?" Jordie asks.

"You heard her. She will unless she thinks she's going to have to tell a lie. And then, believe me, she'll spill her guts."

The bitterness in her sister's voice stuns Jordie. "She's done it before, hasn't she?" she asks.

"She promised not to tell when we booby-trapped Jessica's locker and then ratted us out when Mr. Atherly looked her in the eye and asked her if she knew anything about it."

Jordie doesn't know whether to laugh or cry. She knows Carly and her friends pulled a special kind of detention for that prank—they had to scrub every bathroom and toilet in the school. But this is the first time Jordie has heard how they got busted.

Jordie hopes the police stay away from Deedee. She's almost ready to pray for it.

Sixteen

On Monday morning, the temperature is well below zero. The sun is bright, and there isn't a single cloud in the sky. The snow, knee-deep in places where it hasn't drifted and thigh- or waist-deep in places where it has— is crusted over; if your boots were to crack the surface and plunge down into the soft stuff underneath, you'd have a rough time pulling them out through the same holes. Jordie, standing at her bedroom window, groans at the thought of heading back to school. She does well in all her classes. But she's ready to move on. She knows she's university bound. And she's more than ready for it, having long ago gotten over the thrill of the supposed freedom offered by high school in contrast to the nanny-like teachers and administrators of elementary school and junior high.

Today, her antipathy to high school is more specific. There are things she wants to accomplish today, and school will just get in her way. She considers ditching it altogether, but her homeroom teacher is in her mother's bridge club and is a notorious gossip as well, so would call her mother before midmorning to inquire about Jordie's whereabouts, especially under the circumstances. Jordie can just imagine how the conversation would go: *Poor Jordie, she must be so devastated. I suppose the police have talked to her, seeing as how, well, I suppose she must have been one of the last people to see Derek before he disappeared...*No way. Jordie checks her backpack to make sure she has everything she needs, and off she goes.

Kids, mostly girls, ask her about Derek, which is exactly what she expected would happen. Some of them tear up when they mention his name. A lot of them hug her—even girls she doesn't particularly like and who, she is sure, don't particularly like her. They hug her and say how sorry they are, and how awful it is that someone would do something like that to such a nice guy, and how awful it must be for her, and does she have any idea what happened or who would have done such a thing, and do the police have any idea, have they caught anyone yet, and his poor, poor parents, Derek was their only child, they must be falling apart, just falling apart.

During morning announcements, after Mr. Acheson, the principal, has welcomed everyone back over the PA system, his voice hits a somber note and he informs everyone that they have lost a member of their very own community. Every eye turns to Jordie, and she slumps down in her chair and keeps her focus firmly on her desktop. He announces the funeral, which will take place on Wednesday. Students who knew Derek are encouraged to attend. Students are also reminded that winter carnival is fast approaching and are encouraged, despite this setback in the school community, to attend and partici- pate and, it is hoped, "help to heal the hurt that we are all feeling."

Jordie goes through the motions. She spots Ronan in his normal spot in the last row in her history class, but he manages to slip out the back door as soon as the bell rings. She looks for him at lunchtime, starting at his locker, then in the cafeteria. Then she thinks to go down to the strip mall a few blocks away, where there is a Subway, a pizza joint and a greasy spoon geared to students that does a booming trade in fries and gravy, burgers and chili dogs. She is buttoning her coat, headed for the front doors of the school, when the cops appear. There are two of them, in plain clothes, with long coats and scarves hung around their necks, looking like the homicide cops you see on TV. It's Diehl and Tritt. They stride through the foyer and veer right, clearly making for the school office. Diehl's eyes meet Jordie's. There is no expression on his face. He is all business.

The cops disappear around the corner, and Jordie stops at the front doors. There's no doubt that they're here to ask questions about Derek. Jordie wishes there were some way to find out what they're thinking. But there isn't. She pulls her hat down over her ears and hurries out into the crisp noon air.

Ronan isn't at the Subway. He isn't at the pizza joint. Nor is he at the greasy spoon. She's given up all hope of finding him when she literally collides with him as he comes out of the drugstore, a small white bag in his hand to which is stapled a prescription receipt. He shoves the bag in his pocket when he sees her.

"You want to watch where you're going," he says.

"I've been looking all over for you."

He doesn't smile. He doesn't look flattered the way Derek would if she had collided with him. He just says, "And?"

"The cops are at school."

There is no reaction that she can perceive.

"Ronan—" What is it she wants to say? "Can we talk someplace?"

He's not going to make it easy for her. "About what?"

She glances up and down the street and spots a couple of students from school. "Someplace quiet," she says.

He shrugs and leads her down the block and around the corner. "How about there?" He nods at a kids' park, its swing set minus the swings, its seesaws half frozen to the ground, its whirly-go-round buried in snow. She nods, and they cross the street. Ronan brushes the snow off the crossbar of the seesaws, and they perch side by side.

"So what's up?" he asks.

She looks at him. He's so calm, which should make her feel better. Surely if he had killed Derek, he would be nervous. He'd act evasive. He'd avoid her. He'd avoid everyone.

Except that those things would make him seem suspicious. They would send out warning signals, red flags. Make him a target for investigation. Ronan is smart enough to know that. He's also, in her experience, opaque enough that she can't tell whether he's being genuine with her or putting on an act.

"What if I told you someone saw you and Derek fighting at school just before the holidays?"

She gets absolutely no reaction, even when she looks directly into his eyes. Has he really always been like this and she never noticed? It can't be. She would never have gone out with him if he were this unreadable. Would she?

"Ronan, what if the cops find out?"

"Find out what?"

"That you and Derek were fighting. Weren't you listening to what I just said?"

"So what if they find out? You think that means I killed him?" His eyes bore into hers, and she knows he's having no trouble at all reading her thoughts. "You do, don't you? You think I killed him, and I bet you think I did it because I'm jealous he was going out with you. Is that what you think?"

There's a twist to the words like a knife to the belly, and she knows exactly what he's thinking: *Because that's ridiculous, and you know it. Because if that was how I felt about you, I never would have dumped you in the first place.* Tears well up in her eyes and she wipes them away, hard, with her mitts. They're angry tears, tears of frustration, but she doesn't want him to think they're something else.

"I think it's about that stupid bracelet," she says finally. Angrily. Spitting the words at him and feeling pleased—no, thrilled—when she sees the hurt in his eyes. "I know you were right. I know Derek had it."

Ronan stiffens. "Oh?" His voice is as chilly as the air around them. "So you lied to me before."

A statement, not a question, as if it's the truth.

"I didn't know before," she says and tries to convey the impression that she doesn't care whether he believes her or not. "Carly took it. She thought I wouldn't care since we weren't going out anymore. She took it and sold it to a friend of hers."

"What friend?" He's one hundred percent focused on that bracelet, like it's the only thing he cares about, and she still doesn't know why.

"It doesn't matter. Because that friend sold it to someone else, and that person sold it to Derek when he found out that Derek was looking for something special to give me for an anniversary present."

"Anniversary?"

"Our two-month anniversary." She's aware how ridiculous that sounds to him. Ronan would never celebrate a two-month anniversary. "So you were right. Derek had it."

"I know. I told you that."

She nods. "The thing is, Ronan…" She looks into his eyes again and wishes that the old saying held true in his case, that his eyes were the windows to his soul. But they aren't. She looks into them and all she sees is deep blue. There's nothing behind them—at least, nothing visible to her. "The thing is, the bracelet is missing."

He doesn't say anything.

"I'm pretty sure Derek was going home that night to get it and give it to me. But it's not in his room; I checked. And the police didn't find it on him. Whoever killed Derek didn't take his wallet or even the money that was in it. They didn't take his watch, which was brand new. So I figure if he went home and got the bracelet and was on his way back to my place with it, then whoever killed him must have taken the bracelet from him." She peers into his eyes again, and this time she sees something. Anger. He isn't even trying to hide it.

"You think I just happened to be out in the middle of the night—"

"It could have been the morning. No one knows for sure when he left my house, and because it was so cold, no one knows exactly when he died."

"You think I was out whenever and ran into him—or maybe you think I staked out your house in the hope that he would leave and go home—and I killed him and then stole the bracelet—*my* bracelet—from him. Is that what you think?"

"I don't know what to think, Ronan. I know you wanted the bracelet back." She still has no idea why it was so important to him all of a sudden. "I know you saw Derek with it. I know you almost got into a fistfight with him at school. I know that a button like the ones on your jacket was found right near his body. And I know the bracelet is missing. Someone has it, Ronan, but it's not Derek."

"You think I'm a killer?" He shakes his head. "All that time we were together, I thought you knew me better than that."

"You're kidding, right?" She can't help herself. "All that time we were together and I know practically nothing about you that I didn't know before, which isn't all that much because you never let down your guard, not even for a second. You keep everything inside. You never talk about yourself. You never tell me what's on your mind. I have to guess all the time. It's like you never trusted me. You never trust anyone."

Ronan stands up. She's gotten a reaction out of him, all right. His eyes are like flamethrowers, and she's in their line of fire.

"Did you talk to them?" he asks.

"Who?"

"The police. Did you talk to them? Did you share your little theory with them?"

"No!"

"Not yet, you mean."

"Ronan, I just—"

But he's already turned and is striding across the playground, headed back to the road. She gets up. She starts after him. Then, just as quickly, she stops. What's the point? He's not going to talk to her. He's not going to tell her anything. He never has.

After he walks away from Jordie, Ronan Barthe heads back to school. He doesn't want to go. He hasn't wanted to go in a long time, but now is not the time to draw attention to himself by making himself scarce. If things were different—if, for example, he didn't know the cops were there nosing around—he would ditch the whole thing, go down to the lake, maybe put on his skates and go forever. Well, it would seem like forever. The lake is big. When he was a kid and his mom or his dad read him stories that mentioned the ocean—they said oceans were the largest bodies of water in the world—he thought about the lake where they'd gone one summer. He couldn't imagine anything bigger.

He feels like a fool. When Jordie rammed into him outside the drugstore, when he opened his mouth to snarl at whoever it was and saw that it was her, he felt a jolt zing through him, like a bolt of lightning. There's something about Jordie that makes him go weak in the knees and soft in the head. There always has been. It used to scare him that just looking at a girl could make him feel like that. After they split up—his idea, not hers—the feeling didn't go away, and then he used to curse it and her for the hold she had on him even after he'd decided it was over. For the past couple of months, he's been back where he was before they started going together, before that first time he walked partway home with her and made an effort to talk to her. Back then, every time he saw her, he felt a swoosh of longing and desire shoot through him. He felt it worse when he saw her walking hand in hand with Derek Maugham. He feels it worse than ever now and feels like the world's biggest idiot because of it.

Jordie thinks he killed Derek Maugham.

Okay, maybe she doesn't out-and-out believe it. Maybe she's just afraid he did. She's put together a handful of facts, and when she looks at them and tries to piece them together into something coherent, what she gets is the distinct possibility that he's a murderer. And if *she's* entertaining that notion...

He wonders if the cops know everything she knows. They have the button. She told him that. But do they know whose button it is? Did Jordie tell them? He doesn't think she did—at least, he's pretty sure that when she found him down on the lake and told him about the button, she hadn't told them then. But what about since then?

Did she tell them about the bracelet? That damned bracelet. The only time he ever talked to Maugham was about that bracelet. The only time he ever talked to Jordie after she started going out with Maugham, it was also about that bracelet. That bracelet ties him to Maugham. But who knows that besides Jordie and himself—and Maugham?

And then there's that stupid dustup he had with Maugham before the Christmas break. Jordie says someone saw that. The only person he remembers is Merriwether, and Merriwether didn't see the whole thing. Still, you never know with teachers. If the cops start asking about Maugham, if they ask if he had any trouble with anyone, if he ever fought with anyone, Merriwether might remember the two of them in the hall that day. It wasn't much, but if there is no one else for the cops to focus on, it could turn their attention to Ronan.

So he goes back to school, getting there well before the end of lunch period, and he strolls past the school office at a leisurely pace, casting a glance through the window as he passes. He sees two suits in there—cops for sure. They're talking to Principal Acheson, who is shaking his head. One of the cops raises his head and catches sight of Ronan. Ronan keeps walking.

The announcement comes over the PA system after lunch. The police are asking for cooperation from students and staff. They will be asking to speak to students who knew Derek Maugham with a view to finding out what exactly happened to him. If there are students who are not approached by the police but think they have information that might be useful, they are asked to leave their names at the office so that they can be contacted.

As Ronan moves from class to class that afternoon, at least a couple of kids in each one are sent to the office. They are all kids who used to hang out with Derek, either as teammates or friends. Ronan waits. His name is not called. When he walks by the office at the end of the day, he doesn't see the two cops.

Diehl and Tritt both lean back in uncomfortable wooden chairs in the vice-principal's office, where they have been all afternoon. The last of two dozen students who knew Derek Maugham has just left, and so far they have a big fat zero because, according to everything they've been told, the Maugham kid was well liked, was a star athlete, had a hot girlfriend and was never, to anyone's knowledge, in a fight of any kind.

"I forgot how long the day can be when you're trying to find something—anything—to go on," Diehl says.

Tritt looks at his friend. "Are you sure you want to be doing this, Mike? I mean, after what you've just been through—"

"I can't think of a better way to deal with what I've just been through."

Tritt displays a crooked smile. "Some people would call that denial."

"And some people would say there's nothing wrong with denial under the circumstances. I appreciate your concern, Neil. But work is just what I need right now. It takes my mind off Elise. I can't believe how fast she slipped away from me. This case gives me something to do besides feel sorry for myself, and something to think about besides Elise."

Tritt nods. "So what do you think?"

"What do I think? I think this is what it would be like to try to find out who killed Barry Manilow," Diehl says. "I never heard of a kid so bland he didn't piss off somebody. The stranger-mugger angle is starting to look good to me."

"Yeah, except that nothing was stolen," Tritt says sourly. "There was close to a hundred dollars in cash in the kid's wallet."

Diehl shakes his head. "What kind of kid even carries cash these days? I thought it was all plastic."

"His grandma sent it to him," Tritt says. "She sent him a hundred dollars every Christmas—cash. Through the mail. Do you believe that?"

"Maybe whoever did the kid got scared off before he could get the wallet."

"If that were true, we'd have something by now. If someone scared off a mugger—assuming there was a mugger, and I don't think there was—then whoever scared him off would have seen something."

"Not necessarily. It was snowing," Diehl reminds Tritt.

"Which is one more point against a stranger-on-stranger scenario," Tritt says. "The kid was found in the woods behind his house. It was snowing. We didn't even find him at first because he was so buried in the snow. What kind of mugger goes out in a snowstorm and follows a kid—and remember, you're right about the cash: most kids don't carry it anymore; they're all about debit cards—so what kind of freak would follow a kid into the woods in a snowstorm, supposedly to mug him, and then leave him with his wallet, his cell phone, his watch..."

"Druggie," Diehl says.

Tritt laughs. "Now you're putting me on. You need a fix in the middle of a snowstorm, you do a smash-and-grab and hope for the best. You don't follow a kid who probably doesn't even carry cash into the woods."

Diehl stands up and stretches. "Kind of leaves us at a dead end."

"I think we should come back here tomorrow," Tritt says. "Maybe get all the kids together and make a pitch for information. It's a big school. Stuff probably goes on in the halls all the time. Who knows, maybe one of the rug rats or one of the ghosts saw something."

"Ghosts?"

"The kids who are invisible—the dweebs, the nerds, the geeks. The ones no one pays any attention to. We make a general pitch directly to the kids, you never know who might have seen something."

Diehl is nodding. "Worth a shot," he says. "Come on, let's get out of here."

Tritt stands. "We can grab a beer before we head home. And tonight, when I say home, I mean *mi casa*, Mike. You're having supper with us. Ginette insists. And you know what she's like when you try to cross her."

Diehl smiles. "She's a great cook. It would be my pleasure. Thanks."

Seventeen

Carly Cross glances repeatedly at Deedee Sullivan throughout the surprise assembly, which is being held in shifts so that every student in the school will hear what the two police officers have to say. The cops identify themselves as Sergeant Tritt and Lieutenant Diehl (a whisper goes around at this—Lieutenant Diehl is... was...married to Mrs. Diehl, who died over the holidays—just wandered off in the middle of a snowstorm and never came home again). They tell the students that they are trying to find out what happened to Derek Maugham, but to do that, they need help. They have already talked to a lot of kids who knew Derek, but so far they have no leads in their investigation. Now they want to ask anyone who has any information at all about Derek, even if it doesn't seem important, to please come and talk to them. All information will be confidential. No one has to worry about who says what. The cop who is doing most of the talking, Tritt, says he's sure that if the same thing that happened to Derek happened to any one of them, they would want their entire school to help the police catch whoever did it and make sure that person got punished.

"Are there any questions?" Tritt asks at last.

Carly looks sharply at Deedee, whose head has been bowed the whole time. But it isn't Deedee's hand that shoots up. It's the hand of another kid, a nerdy-looking kid Carly sort of recognizes but barely knows because he is a grade ahead of her.

"What kind of information do you mean?" the kid asks. "I mean, if we didn't know the kid, then what could we know about him?"

"I'm glad you asked that," Tritt says. "I went to a big high school like this one. And I know a lot of stuff goes on outside the classroom—kids fooling around, getting into arguments or scrapes, maybe some kids giving other kids a hard time. Not *every*one sees that stuff. But usually *some*one does—maybe a kid is at his or her locker and he or she sees two kids arguing in an otherwise deserted hall. Or maybe two kids are going at it and you turn the corner and you see them. You see something that no one else sees. Anything like that that involves Derek Maugham is what we're looking for. It might turn out to be nothing—a lot of the things that happen in school turn out to be nothing. But we have the big picture. We haven't released everything we know. So we're the ones who are really in the best position to decide what's important and what isn't. That's why we're here talking to you now. If you heard something or saw something, even if you're not at all sure it means anything, we want to know about it. So you can either come and see us down in the office, where we'll be all day, or you can call the phone number on the flyer that you'll get when you leave the auditorium in a few minutes. It's a Crime Stoppers number. There's no call display on the other end, and no one will ask you for your name. You can stay anonymous if you want to. But please, make the call if you have something to say. We really do need your help."

The cops leave the stage, and Ms. Syros, one of the vice-principals, steps up to the mic. She more or less repeats what Sergeant Tritt has just said and then begins to dismiss them, row by row, cautioning them to "keep it orderly, folks."

Deedee seems in a hurry to leave. Carly grabs her by the arm and hauls her close.

"Remember what you promised my sister," she hisses.

Deedee nods, but her eyes don't meet Carly's, which Carly takes as a bad sign.

"If you want to have any friends at all, you'll keep your promise," Carly says.

"I said if they asked—"

"You said if they asked *you*," Carly hisses. "They didn't ask *you*. They asked everyone. Keep your promise or you'll be sorry."

Deedee nods meekly, and Carly stays with her all the way back to class. The thing is, Carly's not sure why she's helping Jordie. Nor does she understand why Jordie wants Deedee to keep quiet about what she saw. If she had to guess, she'd say Jordie is trying to protect Ronan. Protect him from a murder charge. But that doesn't make sense. Jordie would never protect the person who killed her boyfriend—would she? Maybe she's just afraid the cops will think Ronan was involved. But why would they—unless they had a good reason? Does Jordie think some stupid hallway grudge match between her current and her ex-boyfriends will be seen as a motive for murder? Carly supposes the cops could see it that way, but she watches TV just like anyone else and knows the cops need something stronger than that to get Ronan on a murder charge. So the question is: Is there something else? Does Jordie know what it is? Is she worried about Ronan because she still likes him or because she thinks maybe he did it, maybe he killed Derek?

Carly and the rest of her math class troop back into their classroom and take their seats. Mr. Delisle picks up his chalk and continues to explain the problem he put on the board before the assembly was called. Carly picks up her pencil and copies down what he writes. But Deedee doesn't. Deedee stares down at the blank page of her binder. That worries Carly.

>> >> >>

Carly is leaving school at the end of the day. As she passes the office, she glances inside. She sees the two cops in there; like everyone else, they are getting ready to go home. One is zipping up a leather-covered binder. The other is pulling on his coat. They look tired. They also look discouraged, which probably means they didn't get very far today. Well. Too bad. Carly's sorry about Derek—who isn't? But she can't believe he was killed by someone here at school, no matter what Jordie might think.

She is pulling on her hat when someone breezes by her. He's big and he kicks up a wind, like when an eighteen-wheeler whizzes past Mom's little car on the highway. It's Mr. Merriwether. He throws open the office door and says, "I'm glad I caught you. This probably doesn't mean a thing. In fact, I've been debating all day whether to say anything or not. But just before Christmas, I saw—" The office door swings shut, cutting off the rest of his words.

>> >> >>

Carly is breathless when she gets home. "Jordie! Jordie, are you here?"

Of course she's here. Her boots are on the tray. Her backpack is on the floor in the front hall. Carly kicks off her own boots and races upstairs. She bursts into her sister's room without knocking, startling Jordie, who is listening to music on her iPod and doing what looks like French homework. Her face changes from puzzled to concerned as she takes in Carly, who is breathing hard and still in her coat and hat. Jordie removes her earbuds.

"What's wrong? Did Deedee say something?"

"I don't know. I don't think so. But Mr. Merriwether did." She tells Jordie what she heard and saw.

Jordie grabs her cell phone off her bedside table and punches in a number. She must get no answer, because the next thing that happens is she texts someone.

"Jordie," Carly says. "What's going on? What are you so worried about?"

It's almost dark, and the temperature has dropped the way it has every evening for the past few weeks. Ronan is outside, snow shovel in hand, clearing the driveway, when a car pulls up and two men get out. It's the two cops who were at school that day, making their pitch for people to come forward with anything they know about Derek Maugham. Ronan keeps shoveling as they step over the ridge the snowplow left and walk up the drive toward him.

"Ronan Barthe?" one of the two asks.

Ronan nods.

The cop introduces them—Tritt and Diehl—and says they'd like to ask Ronan a few questions.

"About what?" Ronan says.

"What do you think?" Diehl asks. Ronan supposes he's playing bad cop. "About your friend Derek Maugham."

"He wasn't my friend." Ronan sees no point in lying about that.

"So we gather," Diehl says. "We heard about the scrap you and he had in the hallway at school before Christmas. You want to tell us about that, Ronan?"

Ronan's mind races. He says, "What scrap?" But what he's thinking is, Did Jordie tell them? Did she rat him out to the cops?

"You know what scrap, Ronan," Diehl says. "A witness came forward and told us all about it."

Witness? So it's not Jordie. She wasn't there. So who is this witness? Jordie said someone saw him with Maugham that day, but other than Mr. Merriwether, who didn't see a thing—not really—Ronan doesn't remember anyone else in the hall.

He pretends to think hard. He says, "We were fooling around one day after school, but it wasn't what you'd call a scrap."

"What was it about?" the other cop, Tritt, asks.

"What was what about?"

"You said you were fooling around. How did that go? What did you say? What did he say?"

Ronan stares at the cop, incredulous. "I don't remember. It was, like, two weeks ago."

"Well, you just told us he wasn't your friend. So I'm wondering what two guys who aren't friends fool around about at school. Fooling around is usually something you do with your buddies, isn't it? Not with the guy who's going out with your ex-girlfriend. Am I right?" Tritt is talking to Ronan nice and slow, like he's got all the time in the world and this is just a friendly conversation, but he's got his eyes fixed hard on him, trying to read him.

"He's not my friend as in I don't hang out with him. But I know him. He's in a couple of my classes. I see him around."

"In the hall?" Tritt says.

"Yeah."

"So, what happened? You were walking down the hall and you ran into him and you said, 'Hey, how's it going?' Or was he the one who talked first?"

"I don't remember."

"Maybe he said something about your girlfriend," the other cop, Diehl, says. Tritt fishes in his pocket for something. A small flashlight. He flicks it off and on while Diehl says, "I've met her. She's pretty. I bet Derek was having a great time with her. Did he tell you that? Did he tell you how much he was enjoying your girlfriend?"

Ronan has to remind himself that they're on some kind of fishing expedition. If they had something on him, something at least semi-solid, they'd have had him down at the police station by now.

"She's not my girlfriend," he says calmly. "We broke up. And for the record, I'm the one who ended it, not her. You can ask her."

The two cops stare at him. Tritt has the flashlight on again, and he's got it aimed at Ronan. He's running it up and down the front of Ronan's jacket, and Ronan is trying not to show the immense relief he feels at having sewn on a new button to replace the one that was missing.

"Where were you the night Derek Maugham got killed?" Tritt asks, shutting off the flashlight and dropping it back into his pocket.

"What night was that exactly?"

"You don't know?"

"I didn't even know he was dead until someone told me."

"And who was that?"

No way, Ronan thinks. "I don't remember."

Tritt looks long and hard at him before telling him when Maugham was reported missing.

"Where were you that night, Ronan?"

Ronan takes a few seconds. He's never bought those cop shows where people remember instantly where they were and what they were doing at a specific time a week or two weeks or even a month ago. Sure, if you happened to be at some special event, or doing something like, say, writing a test or celebrating someone's birthday, you might remember. But mostly, life is just more of the same day after day and night after night, and sameness is the beige of life—you can't tell where one piece of it ends and the next piece begins.

"I was at home, I guess," he says at last.

"You guess?"

"I was home most of the holidays. I worked during the day and chilled at night."

"Can anyone verify that, Ronan?"

"Maybe my mom. She's always home. But she's sick, so she sleeps a lot." It's lame, and he knows it. But it also has the ring of being reasonable if not true. He holds his breath. The two cops look him over, trying to give him the impression they're soul readers. But in the end all they do is thank him for his time—it doesn't sound remotely sincere—and go back to their car. Ronan keeps shoveling while they drive away. He's pretty sure they don't notice how badly his hands are shaking.

Eighteen

The church is packed, which comes as no surprise to Jordie. Practically the whole school is there. So is everyone who knows Derek's parents—and that's a lot of people. The Maughams have lived in town forever. Mrs. Maugham grew up here. Mr. Maugham came up here as the result of a bank transfer. He has risen steadily through the ranks and is now in charge of all of his bank's branches in the district. Everyone in business knows him. So do a lot of people who've had mortgages and loans approved by him over the years. And it goes without saying that a man in his business is active in the local service club and at a local church, that he sits on the boards of a number of non-profits and that he turns out for every pancake breakfast, every fundraiser, every children's sports tournament and every fall fair held in the town and/or environs.

So, of course, everyone who has ever met him or done business with him or benefited from the donations handed out by his bank shows up at his son's funeral. Not that it's just a matter of being practical. People genuinely feel for him. What parent wouldn't? After all, isn't every parent's nightmare that they will outlive their children?

Mr. Maugham sits up front, tall and straight. If he cries, there are no signs of it later, when he follows the casket down the aisle. Mrs. Maugham is another matter. She weeps throughout the service. Mr. Maugham makes no attempt to quiet her. He puts his arm around her shoulder and leaves it there the whole time. His arm is still there when they walk down the aisle together behind the casket.

People file out of the church slowly, pausing in the vestibule to say a few words to the Maughams. A reception is being held in the church hall, but not everyone will stay for that, so those who must hurry back to their offices or classrooms take the opportunity to express their sympathy. Jordie joins the line. After all, she was Derek's girlfriend. But her courage wavers when, third from the front of the line, she catches Mrs. Maugham looking at her. Glaring at her, really, her tears dried now, her mouth set in a firm line. The person who was speaking to her moves on, and now Jordie is second in line. The person in front of her, a woman from the church, grasps Mrs. Maugham's hand and says how sorry she is and what a wonderful boy Derek was. Mrs. Maugham doesn't look at the woman. Her eyes are on Jordie.

Jordie tries to bear up. She tells herself that no matter what, she owes it to Derek to say a few kind words to his mother. So when the church woman moves on, Jordie steps forward. She tells Mrs. Maugham it was a nice service and that it's wonderful so many people showed up and that it must be a comfort to know so many people cared about Derek and miss him. Mrs. Maugham doesn't say anything, and where before she stared at Jordie, now she refuses to look at her, and for some reason this hurts Jordie worse than anything Mrs. Maugham could say. At least, that's what she thinks as she steps sideways to tell Mr. Maugham how sorry she is. Mr. Maugham grasps her hand. He thanks her for coming, and Jordie is grateful to him. Then, as she moves on, she hears Mrs. Maugham's voice. She is talking to another mourner: "None of this would have happened if the girl he was seeing, that Jordana Cross, hadn't taken it into her head to have a fight with him. That's what drove him out of her house that night. She admitted it to me herself."

Jordie turns and looks at Mrs. Maugham and is shocked to see the woman looking triumphantly at her, as if daring her to protest. Mostly, Jordie wants to cry. But she doesn't. She doesn't say a word either—what use would it be? And what would people think if she got into an argument with Mrs. Maugham, the poor grieving mother of a poor murdered boy, right here at the church doors on the very day of the funeral while the coffin sits just there, waiting to be taken away and stored somewhere—Jordie doesn't want to think where—until the ground thaws and he can be buried in the cemetery where all of Mrs. Maugham's family has been buried for three generations, or is it four?

Jordie scurries outside and watches people leave, waiting for some of the kids from her class or for Carly, for anybody, really, to walk back to school with. Kids stream out. Not many have stopped and talked to the Maughams. Not many want to put themselves through that. Jordie knows what they're thinking because she's heard them say it out loud: What are you supposed to say? What if you say something that makes them more upset? What if you make them cry?

They come out in twos and threes, in clumps and bunches, and even though Jordie knows most of them, she doesn't join any of the groups. She's waiting, she realizes, for one specific person. That person never walks down the church steps. Only when Mr. and Mrs. Maugham come out, followed closely by the minister, and take the neatly shoveled path to the church hall does Jordie know for sure what she has been thinking all along: Ronan did not come to the funeral. She tells herself it's understandable—he didn't know Derek well, or, really, at all. He had no reason to like him. Why would he come? Still, it seems wrong.

Maybe that's why Jordie finds herself at the hardware store after school. Mr. Sorenson, the owner, greets her like a long-lost daughter. She used to stop by here all the time when she and Ronan were together. She went by almost every day in the summer, on her lunch break, and she and

Ronan would eat their sandwiches together at the picnic table beside the parking lot.

"You stopped coming by all of a sudden," Mr. Sorenson says now. "I asked Ronan about you a couple of times, but all he did was shrug. I had to find out from my daughter"—who is the same age as Jordie—"that you two split up."

"Is he here?"

Mr. Sorenson shakes his head. "He works Thursday and Friday nights and all day Saturday during school."

She thanks him and decides to go home. What would she say to Ronan anyway? But her feet somehow carry her far past her street and all the way to his. The first thing she sees when she turns the corner is police cars. Two are parked on the street. Two more have pulled into Ronan's driveway. As she walks up the street, staring at the squad cars, she sees that there are police officers at four different houses, talking to people at their front doors. One of the cops leaves a house two doors up from Ronan's but on the other side of the street. He walks directly to Ronan's house and goes inside without ringing the bell. He's back out again a moment later with Lieutenant Diehl. He is telling Diehl something. Then he points at the house he has just left. Diehl starts across the street. He goes directly to the house the cop pointed to, rings the bell and talks to the man who answers. He waves to the uniformed cop, who hurries to join Diehl. All three men talk. Then Diehl strides across the street and goes back into Ronan's house. A few minutes later, two more uniformed officers, who must have already been inside the house, come out. Ronan is between them. He is in handcuffs. The cops put him in a squad car and drive away. Diehl and Tritt come out a few minutes later. They get into an unmarked car and drive away. Jordie doesn't know what to think. She stands out in the street, all but oblivious to all the faces at all the windows, until the cold permeates her to the core. Only then does she head home.

There's nothing on the news that night. But it's on the morning show her mother has on in the kitchen while she cooks breakfast the next morning, and it's in the newspaper her father reads before he goes to work.

"They made an arrest in Derek's murder case," Mrs. Cross says. Her face is a map of concern. "They're not saying who it is because the person is under eighteen." She looks significantly at Jordie. "Do you think it's someone from your school?"

"How would I know that, Mom?" Jordie doesn't want to discuss this with her mother. She doesn't want to hear her mother's opinion of Ronan.

"How would you know what?" Carly, always annoyingly chipper in the morning, has bounced into the kitchen and snatched a piece of her father's buttered toast.

"I was just telling your sister that the police arrested someone for Derek's murder—a young person," Mrs. Cross says.

Jordie shoots her sister a poisonous look. But Carly doesn't notice. She doesn't say anything about Ronan either. Instead, all she says is, "I guess the gossip mill will be working overtime at school today. Are you making more toast, Mom?"

Jordie eats some cereal and drinks some coffee as if this were an ordinary day. But her mind is racing and it takes all of her willpower not to dash out of the house and…and what? She wants to know what's going on with Ronan. She wants to know what the police know—are they 100 percent sure that he did it? Do they even have to be 100 percent sure? Beyond a reasonable doubt—isn't that the way juries are supposed to look at it? She wishes she'd paid more attention in her law course last year. She knows that probable cause is the big thing the police have to take into consideration. But what exactly is the difference between probable cause and reasonable doubt? Is she even remembering it right?

Say the police are sure Ronan is the killer. What have they based that on? What did that man across the street tell them? Who else talked to them about Ronan? And what about physical evidence? That's supposed to be the most important thing. That she does remember. People can be mistaken, or they can lie. But physical evidence is supposed to be objective. DNA is what it is. A fingerprint or a bloodstain or a tire track—they are what they are. So what's the physical evidence in Ronan's case?

Jesus. He's been arrested for murder. She can't believe it, even if it's one of the things she's been worrying about ever since she saw that button. But who can tell her what it's all about? Who can tell her what they have? The only person she can think of is Ronan, and what are the chances that she will even be allowed to see him? If he's been arrested, and if the charge is murder, then he'll be held until his trial date. She's pretty sure she has that right. And he won't be held in town. There are no youth facilities here. He'll be held a hundred miles away. She can maybe try to visit him, but she isn't sure how that works. She can't believe it. She can't believe any of it.

Everyone is talking about the arrest at school. Everyone is speculating about who it is. Then she hears someone say it flat-out: "It's Ronan Barthe."

"How do you know that?" she demands.

The kid who said it, a jock friend of Derek's named Brendan Roark, says, "Because Mr. Merriwether told the cops he caught them fighting in the hall."

This, Jordie knows, is a lie. Mr. Merriwether didn't actually see a fight. He saw Ronan with a homicidal look in his eyes—isn't that what Deedee said? Still, she's not surprised the word is out that Mr. Merriwether talked to the cops and that it had something to do with Ronan and Derek. Jordie has never figured out exactly how it happens, but everything eventually gets out. This is no exception.

"And everyone knows how that creep Barthe felt about Derek, especially after you started going with him." There's an edge to the words, and the look on Brendan's face isn't remotely friendly, never mind sympathetic. He's blaming me, Jordie realizes. He thinks Derek is dead because of me.

She doesn't argue with him. She doesn't want to get into it, doesn't want to hear him say flat-out what he's already implying, doesn't want to hear how long it takes for *that* to get around, assuming it hasn't already. She walks on, into the school and up to her locker.

Nobody says anything to her face about it being her fault or about Ronan's jealousy being the motive for what happened to Derek. Neither does anyone ask her if she knows whether it's true that Ronan is the one who was arrested. Why should they? He's obviously missing from school. He obviously had a reason to dislike Derek. And he's not one of the in kids. He doesn't play sports. He doesn't talk much. He's not much of a joiner. And he's only been in town for a little over a year. No one really knows him. When you get right down to it, Jordie barely knows him.

There is only one person she can think of to talk to. Ronan's mother.

The whole time Jordie went out with Ronan, she never met his mother. He never wanted to take her back to his house. He never offered to introduce her, and she assumed he wasn't on good terms with her. For some reason, that seems to jibe with what she knows about Ronan. He did mention that his dad was "out of the picture." The contempt in his voice was palpable when he said it. Bad divorce, she thinks. A dad who never shows up when it is his day or weekend or whatever to be with Ronan. Maybe a dad who doesn't pay child support. And who knows, maybe a mother who doesn't cope well with that. For all she knows, maybe a mother on welfare. Or an alcoholic mother. Or just a pathetic mother. It all adds up to the same thing: Jordie is nervous about approaching her. But does she have any choice?

She takes her time going up the walk. She wonders how to introduce herself. As a friend of Ronan's? As his ex-girlfriend? As someone who cares what happens to him? For sure, not as Derek Maugham's girlfriend.

She reaches the door and presses the bell. A woman answers.

"Mrs. Barthe?" Jordie says. "I'm Jordie Cross. I—"

"Whoa. Hold up, honey. I'm not Mrs. Barthe. I'm the home-care nurse."

Nurse?

"Is—is Mrs. Barthe here?"

The nurse, a squat, barrel-shaped woman in stretch pants and a Christmas sweater, nods as she looks Jordie over.

"Do you think I can see her?" Jordie asks.

"Does she know you, honey?"

"I'm a friend of her son's. Of Ronan's."

"Uh-huh," the nurse says, clearly suspicious. "That phone in there has been ringing off the hook with reporters." She looks up and down the street over Jordie's shoulder. "How do I know you're not one of them or that one of them hasn't sent you here to get some information?"

"You can tell her my name. Jordie Cross."

"Oh, so she *does* know you?" Still skeptical.

"I used to go out with her son. I—we're still friends."

The woman snorts. Still, she says, "Okay. Tell you what. You stay here, and I'll go and ask her if she wants to see you." Before Jordie can say anything, the door closes in her face. She waits.

And waits.

She waits so long that she begins to wonder if the nurse is ever coming back. She begins to feel like an idiot, freezing her butt off on the stoop.

The door opens again.

"She said okay." The nurse opens the door wide enough for Jordie to squeeze through. "She's upstairs. I'm giving you ten minutes. The poor thing is exhausted as it is."

Jordie pulls off her boots and hat and unbuttons her coat. She climbs the stairs to the second floor.

"Front of the house," the nurse calls after her.

Jordie heads for the door to the front bedroom. She taps on it.

The voice that answers is thin and reedy. "Come in."

Jordie steps into the master bedroom, its double bed empty and tightly made (by the nurse, Jordie guesses), its occupant seated in a wheelchair in front of the window, an oxygen tank at her side and an oxygen-intake tube strapped around her head. The woman is painfully thin, shockingly pale and has deep circles around her sunken eyes. She is wearing a housecoat that seems much too large for her and enormous, fluffy slippers.

"Mrs. Barthe?"

The woman looks her up and down. "So you're the famous Jordie." Her voice is a bare whisper. "Ronan is right. You're very pretty." She lifts a hand and gestures weakly to an ottoman at the foot of the bed. "Sit."

Jordie sits. Mrs. Barthe is seriously ill, there's no doubt about that. Why didn't Ronan ever mention that?

"What can I do for you, Jordie?"

"It's about Ronan."

Mrs. Barthe nods. "Of course." She is breathing hard every time she speaks. Now she coughs. It seems a chore for her to stop, and Jordie doesn't know what to do to help her.

"My water," Ronan's mother manages to say. She nods to a drinking bottle with a straw sticking out of it. Jordie rises to get it. She is about to hand it to Mrs. Barthe, who has raised her arm to reach for it. But she freezes. Her eyes are on the bracelet around Mrs. Barthe's wrist. It's the same one Ronan gave Jordie. Jordie's sure of it. It's not just similar. It's the exact same one.

Mrs. Barthe is coughing as if she's going to choke. She manages to croak a single word: "Water."

Jordie comes back to herself. She hands her the water and watches her suck greedily on the straw. She waits until the bottle is handed back to her. She sets it down and then sits again. But her mind is on that bracelet. It's the same one; she knows it is. But how did Ronan get his hands on it?

There is only one way she can think of.

"You like the bracelet?" Mrs. Barthe asks.

"It's beautiful."

Mrs. Barthe holds out her arm and admires it. "Yes, it is. It was a gift from my husband—in much happier days, of course. It's the one thing about his father that Ronan doesn't disapprove of. But that's because Ronan picked it out, although I didn't find that out until a couple of weeks ago."

Oh? thinks Jordie.

"When his father walked out on me, I was bitter. I admit it. I threw the bracelet in the trash." She fingers it fondly. "Ronan never said a word, but I imagine he was crushed." She holds out her wrist and shows Jordie the familiar, delicate patterns in the silver. "Honeysuckle for true love, ivy for love, forget-me-not for fidelity and, of course, roses for one love. Ronan found it at a one-of-a-kind craft show. When Doug—my ex-husband—told me about it, I apologized to Ronan. He presented this to me a few days after Christmas. It turns out he'd found it in the trash and rescued it." She smiles, but Jordie has never seen a person look as weary as Mrs. Barthe looks. "I'm glad." She looks up. "So, Jordie, what can I do for you?"

"It's about Ronan. I was hoping to be able to see him."

"He's been arrested. Did you know that?"

Jordie nods.

"And what do you think?" Mrs. Barthe asks. Tired or not, her eyes are sharp as they search Jordie's. "Do you think he murdered that boy?"

Jordie doesn't know what she thinks. She only knows what she fears. But if she wants Mrs. Barthe's help, she knows she has to stay on her side.

"Ronan doesn't seem like the kind of person who would ever hurt another person on purpose," she says finally.

This earns another smile from Mrs. Barthe, but this one is enigmatic and just a little bit sad. Mrs. Barthe does not say what *she* thinks.

"His lawyer phoned about an hour ago," she says instead. "He had given me to believe that it is next to impossible to get bail for a person who has been charged with murder." Jordie knows this. "But he said that given the circumstances—" She looks Jordie in the eye. "What I mean is, given *my* circumstances, the judge, over the objections of the Crown, has agreed to let Ronan come home for the time being, on the condition that he wear one of those ankle things that will set off an alarm if he leaves the house and that he submit to daily visits from the police, at their discretion with regard to time and frequency, to check on him. Part of me is afraid to have him home."

Jordie frowns.

"Not afraid *of* him," Mrs. Barthe clarifies. "Afraid *for* him. I may be seriously ill, but I'm no fool. I know what people think. And I know what people who are blinded by hate can do. He might be safer locked up somewhere. But if they lock him up, I might never see him again. Quite a dilemma, don't you think?"

Jordie takes in the oxygen tank, the alarming thinness of the woman's face and arms, the pallor of her skin, the manlike shortness of her hair. Why didn't Ronan tell her?

"Can you ask him to call me, Mrs. Barthe? It's important."

"Of course. Now, if you'll excuse me, I'm very tired. Could you please ask Renee—the nurse—to come up here?"

Jordie stands. She thanks Ronan's mother again. When she reaches the bottom of the stairs, she delivers the message to the nurse, who insists on seeing Jordie out first.

Why didn't he tell me, Jordie wonders again as she makes her way down the front walk. She is almost at the corner of the street when a police squad car slides by. Ronan is in the backseat. He turns his head to look at her as the car goes by. She stops. The car pulls into

Ronan's driveway. Two cops get out. One of them opens the back door of the car, and Ronan steps out. His hands are behind his back. He is handcuffed, Jordie realizes. Handcuffed, but home.

Nineteen

Jordie stands on the corner until she is shivering. She wonders how long it will take Mrs. Barthe to deliver her message to Ronan—*if* she delivers it.

Her phone buzzes in her pocket.

She snatches it and answers without checking the display.

"Jordie."

"Dad?"

"Where are you?"

"I'm—" She can't tell the truth. Not now. "I'm on my way home."

"Tell me exactly where you are. I'll pick you up."

Jordie is already walking as she answers. She doesn't know why her father sounds so anxious, but she's pretty sure his mood won't be improved by finding out where she is standing.

"I'm on Clearwater," she says, and, sure enough, by the time she says it, she is. "What's wrong?"

"Clearwater and what?"

"Clearwater walking toward home."

"Okay. I'm getting in the car right now. Keep walking. I'll find you."

"Okay. But Dad—"

Too late. He's rung off.

She quickens her pace, determined to get as far from Ronan's street as she can before her father's car appears. She is sweaty and huffing but six blocks farther by the time the car appears around a corner. He stops next to her and leans across to shove open the passenger-side door.

"Get in."

She's still buckling up when he pulls away from the curb.

"What's wrong, Dad? Did something happen?"

"The police called, that's what happened." He takes his eyes off the road for a second to peer into his daughter's eyes. He does not look pleased.

"And?"

"Those two detectives want to talk to you, Jordie."

"I already talked to them."

"They want to talk to you again."

"Okay." Is her dad worried? Is that the expression she sees on his face? Or is it something else?

They drive in silence for a minute.

"Carly says Ronan stopped by the house the night Derek left."

That little rat. Jordie is going to get back at her if it's the last thing she does.

"Carly wasn't the one who told the police, so you can wipe that look off your face, young lady," her father says. "Apparently she mentioned it to Tasha, who, after what happened, mentioned it to her parents, who called the police, who then called me." He sounds exasperated. "Why didn't you say something about this earlier? And exactly what was that boy doing at our house?"

"He wanted to ask me something."

"He hasn't heard of the telephone? He couldn't text you or Facebook you or whatever the preferred method of communication is among young people these days?"

"I don't know, Dad. All I know is that he came by to ask me something."

"What?"

The cops were going to ask her the same question. She needed to come up with a good answer. But what?

"I'm waiting, Jordie." Her dad is slow-burn impatient now.

"I had some stuff of his from when we were going out. He wanted it back."

Her father glances at her again.

"What stuff?" The dryness in his voice implies skepticism.

"A sweater. A navy-blue sweater. The big wooly one. You know the one, Dad. You make a comment every time I wear it."

"That humongous thing that looks like a sack on you?"

She nods.

"That belongs to Ronan?"

Another nod.

"What the hell are you doing wearing your ex-boyfriend's sweater?"

"It's warm. It's like wearing a woolen blanket. And it's so soft."

"But it belongs to Ronan."

"I know."

"Did you give it back?"

"Not yet. I've been wearing it for ages. I told him I would wash it and then return it, but with everything that's happened, I haven't got around to it yet."

"Okay," her father says. "Well, if that's all it is—"

"What else would it be, Dad?"

"Why didn't you tell the police he'd been by?"

"I didn't think it was relevant. Why? Do you think it means anything?"

"He may have seen that Derek was there. It may have set him off."

Jordie bets the cops will think the same thing. But maybe after she tells them what really happened between her and Ronan, they will change their minds—that is, if they believe her.

>> >> >>

Just like the last time, the two detectives thank her for
coming down to speak to them. This time, though,
there's no softness as they go through her rights, which
Tritt reads off a sheet of paper, pointing to where she's to
initial that she understands and agrees. Does she understand that she doesn't have to answer any questions if she
doesn't want to? Does she understand that anything she
does choose to say can be used against her in a subsequent
legal proceeding?

"Wait a minute!" her dad says. "What legal proceeding?
Are you charging her with anything?"

"Not at this time," Diehl says.

Her father doesn't like the sound of that. "Maybe I
should get a lawyer down here."

"It's okay, Dad," Jordie says, laying a hand on her
father's arm. "I don't need a lawyer. I didn't do anything."

Her father's arm is tense, but he says nothing.

Jordie nods at Tritt, who reads the next paragraph on
the sheet.

Does she understand that she can choose to have a
lawyer present? Does she understand that she can choose
to have a parent present?

"Damn straight she does, Neil," her father mutters.
He gives Tritt the stinkeye.

Jordie initials the box Tritt points to. He sets the
paper aside.

"Okay, Jordie. There are a few things that we need your help with. Things we need clarified."

"Like what?" Jordie uses her sweetest classroom voice.

"For example, we find it odd that you didn't tell us that Ronan Barthe came to your house and spoke to you the same night you say Derek Maugham left your house and never came back."

The same night that she *says* Derek left? Whoa!

"I don't remember you asking me about Ronan." She smiles cooperatively. "But, yes, he did drop by. He wanted something of his that I still have. We used to go out."

"What did he want?"

"A sweater." Jordie gives the two cops an abbreviated version of the story she told her father.

"Derek Maugham was at your house at the time, isn't that right, Jordie?" Tritt asks.

"That's right."

"Did he know that Ronan was there?"

"Yes."

"Did Derek talk to Ronan?"

"No."

"Any reason why not?"

Was he kidding? "They don't know each other very well. And, well, to be honest, I don't think Derek liked Ronan very much, you know, because he used to be my boyfriend."

"What about Ronan? How does he feel about Derek?"

"I don't think he thinks anything one way or another."

"He wasn't angry or resentful of the guy who stole his girl?"

Jordie shakes her head. "Derek didn't steal me. I was going out with Ronan. Ronan broke up with me. Then I started going out with Derek."

"Ronan dumped you?" Tritt seems to be trying this out to see how it feels.

"He broke up with me," Jordie says.

"Why?"

A good question.

"To be honest," she says, "I don't know. He didn't tell me. He just said he thought it would be best if we didn't see each other anymore."

"Did you ask him why he said that?"

Only about a hundred times.

"Yes. But he wouldn't tell me."

There is silence for a few moments. Jordie can't decipher its meaning.

"Jordie, did you leave your house that night—the night you say Derek left without telling anyone?"

Beside Jordie, her father bridles. She squeezes his arm.

"No."

"You didn't perhaps leave together? Maybe you were going back to his house with him? Maybe you figured that, that way, the two of you could have some privacy?" Tritt asks.

"What exactly are you implying?" Jordie's father demands.

"It's okay, Dad," Jordie says. "No, I didn't go with him. I told you, I didn't even realize he had left the house until the next morning."

"Yet, according to his mother, you knew exactly what route he had taken home, and you were able to find him when no one else could, even after we had search parties out looking," Tritt says. "And you also snuck into his room behind his mother's back after he was dead. What were you doing in there, Jordie?"

Mrs. Maugham had made a point of telling the cops that? God, what else had she said?

"Jordie, is this true?" her father asks.

Jordie looks at the cops, not her dad.

"I was trying to be helpful when I told her the way he usually walks home from our house," she says. "And it was pure luck I happened to see his scarf that day. And about his room—I did *not* go in there behind anyone's back. Mrs. Maugham wasn't there when I went over. I asked Mr. Maugham for permission. I wanted a keepsake of Derek, that's all. You can ask Mr. Maugham if you don't believe me."

The two cops stare at her. She doesn't flinch. What *are* they implying?

"Did you get a keepsake?" Tritt asks at last.

"No. His mother wouldn't let me. She threw me out."

Tritt leans forward across the table. "Do you know what Mrs. Maugham thinks, Jordie?"

Jordie shakes her head, even though she knows exactly what Derek's mom thinks.

"She thinks that you lured Derek out of the house and that you met up with Ronan Barthe, and that Ronan—or both of you—killed Derek and buried his body in the snow."

"She's insane!" Jordie's father says. "That woman doesn't know the first thing about my daughter. She—"

Tritt lays a clear plastic bag on the table. Inside is a metal button. A military-style button. Both Jordie and her dad stare at it. Both are silent.

"Do you recognize this button, Jordie?"

She feels her dad's eyes on her. "A police officer showed it to me when they found Derek," she says.

"What about before that?"

"No."

"What would you say if I told you that Ronan Barthe has a jacket that has buttons exactly like this one?" Tritt asks.

"Are you kidding?" her father says. "Do you have any idea how many of those jackets there must be kicking around, all with buttons like that?"

Tritt and Diehl ignore him.

"What would you say," Tritt continues, "if I told you that one of the buttons on Ronan's jacket had recently been replaced?"

Jordie doesn't answer. What could she possibly say?

"Where were you the night Derek Maugham supposedly went missing?" Tritt asks her again.

"I was home." It's getting harder and harder for Jordie to stay calm—to not panic.

"Can anyone vouch for that?"

"I was asleep. Everyone was asleep."

"Jordie, if you had anything to do with what happened to Derek Maugham, you should tell us," Tritt says.

"I didn't." She glances at Diehl. Why isn't he saying anything?

"Maybe you didn't know what Ronan was planning to do. But with his record—"

"Record?" Jordie and her dad say simultaneously. "What record?" Jordie asks.

"He didn't tell you he'd been arrested twice before—for assault?"

Jordie shakes her head. He'd never said a word about it.

"A boy with a temper like that, he might have surprised you by what he did. He might have told you that since you were there, you were just as much to blame as him. But that's not necessarily true, Jordie. Not if you cooperate. Not if you tell us exactly what happened."

"I don't know what you're talking about," Jordie says. She is thinking about Ronan's record. What kind of assault? Assault on whom? How bad was it?

"If you don't cooperate," Tritt continues, "and if it turns out you've been lying to us—"

Mr. Cross stands up. "Now you're threatening my daughter?"

"We're just trying to figure this out, Art."

"Is she under arrest? Are you arresting her?"

Tritt looks at Diehl, who shakes his head.

"Come on, Jordie," her father says. "We're going home." He grabs her hand before she can say a word and yanks her out of the chair and out of the room. No one tries to stop them.

Jordie's dad says nothing on the way home, which could be good—he's not accusing her of anything, he doesn't seem to be buying the cops' version of events, and he probably doesn't think she could ever do anything even remotely like what they have suggested. But it isn't necessarily all good. He's definitely worried, he'll probably get her a lawyer as fast as he can, and he might not sleep well knowing, just as she does, that some cops are like dogs with a bone. They get an idea into their heads and there's just no shaking them, and believe it or not, we live in a world where the innocent are sometimes punished for the crimes of the guilty—hell, sometimes they're punished for things that aren't crimes at all.

As soon as they get home and he parks the car in the garage, her father walks through the kitchen and into the den, where, shortly thereafter, Jordie hears the clink of glass on glass. Her father is pouring himself a stiff drink.

In the kitchen, Celia Cross searches her daughter's face.

"They didn't arrest me," Jordie says, trying to keep things light.

"Well, I should hope not." Her mother is indignant. She hears the same clinking Jordie hears, frowns and hurries into the den. Jordie hears hushed voices.

She shucks her coat, checks her phone for messages—there are none—and heads up to her room. She's back down five minutes later when her mother calls the family for dinner. Everyone, even Carly, eats in silence. Mr. Cross brings his Scotch—his second?—to the table and drinks it while ignoring the casserole on his plate.

"Damn cops," he mutters.

"Now, Art," Mrs. Cross says softly.

"Don't 'now Art' me! You weren't there. They all but accused your daughter of murder!"

"No shit?" Carly says, wide-eyed.

Both her parents glower at her. "Language," her mother says sharply.

"Sorry," Carly mutters.

"They weren't serious, Mom," Jordie says. "I think they were just trying to scare me."

"Why would they do that?"

"They just want to see if I know anything."

"Well, of course you don't." Her eyes go to her husband. "It's nothing to worry about, is it, Art?" Even though Jordie has just told her it isn't.

"I'm going to call Paul," Mr. Cross says. He stands. "His brother is a prosecutor in Vancouver. He probably knows a lot of good lawyers. I'm going to get one for Jordie."

"But if she didn't do anything, surely she doesn't need a lawyer," Mrs. Cross says.

Mr. Cross picks up his glass to take with him. "Don't be so naïve, Celia," he says. "These are cops. Who knows what they think?"

He disappears into the den again.

Jordie offers to clean up the kitchen, but her mother shoos her away.

"You've dealt with enough for one day. Go and try to relax. Carly will help me."

"Aw, Mom—"

"You'll do as you're told, young lady," her mother says.

Jordie goes to her room. She shuts the door and props a chair under the handle so that she will be warned if someone tries to come in. She turns on her computer.

Twenty

After nearly an hour of staring at the screen of her laptop, Jordie is about to give up. Then Ronan's face appears. He looks tired. Worried, too, and that scares Jordie.

"I saw you on the street," he says. "My mom says you were at the house."

"Are you okay, Ronan?"

"Yeah," he mutters. But he refuses to look into the camera.

"Was it the button? Is that what did it?"

His head bobs up. He peers past her. "How do I know you're alone in there? How do I know someone else isn't hiding there or you aren't recording this or something?"

"You want me to come over? You could search me."

He shakes his head. His eyes meet hers. "What do you want?"

"I'm worried about you, Ronan."

He says nothing.

"The cops brought me in for questioning." Still nothing. "They know you were here that night. They wanted to know what you were doing here."

"Did you tell them?"

"I said you wanted me to return that sweater of yours."

"What sweater?"

"The blue one. You know, the really soft one."

He smiles until he catches himself at it. "*You* have it?"

She nods.

"Huh. I wondered where it had got to."

"You can have it back if you want."

Another tiny smile. "You can keep it."

Silence.

"Ronan? They told me they know that button is yours. They say you sewed another one on to replace it."

"I'm such an idiot. I used a different color thread. And the one they found—it still has some thread attached, the same color as the other ones."

"So it is your button?"

"Yeah."

Silence.

"You want to tell me what it was doing next to where they found Derek?"

"What difference does it make? I can't prove it. And the cops have made up their minds already. We don't have a lot of money, Jordie. I'll probably have to go with a

NORAH McCLINTOCK

legal-aid lawyer, and that's not good. I just hope it doesn't go to trial until after my mother..." His voice trails off. He's looking down again, not at her.

She doesn't know what to say. Should she ask about his mother? Or should she stick to the main event—the question of the button?

"How did the button get there, Ronan?"

Nothing.

"Part of their theory is that you killed him because you were jealous of him—you know, on account of me."

"They've got that right," he mumbles.

"What? What did you say?" She prays to God it isn't what she thinks.

"I am—was—jealous. I admit it."

"But you—"

"Made a big mistake when I broke up with you? I sure did. But I didn't kill Derek. I would never do anything like that."

Never? She wants to ask about the assault convictions he has.

"Jordie, there's something I never told you." He shakes his head. "There's a lot of stuff I never told you."

She waits.

"I got into some trouble before my mom and I moved here. The cops are making a big deal out of it. They're acting like I have this huge temper and I take it out on people. But it's not like that. That isn't what happened."

She's holding her breath.

"My mom is really sick. She has been for a while. But this time, she's not going to make it. She knows it and I know it." She detects a quaver in his voice. He clears his throat noisily, as if to chase it away. "My dad—he decided he couldn't handle it. I love it. My mom has cancer, she's going to die, and *he* can't handle it. So yeah, I guess you could say I assaulted him. I even guess you could say I wanted to kill him, the miserable prick. He pressed charges. And then there was this kid at my old school—we never got along, and when he heard what my dad did...well, when he opened his mouth about that, I couldn't help it. So yeah, I did that stuff. But that's not me, not really. And now they're going to send me to prison and my mom is going to be all alone. Jesus, Jordie, this is going to kill her."

Ronan shifts his gaze away from the computer screen and down to the keyboard of his laptop. He fights to regain control of his emotions. He feels as if that's all he's been doing for the past few days, pretty much ever since he went over to Jordie's house and saw that Maugham was there. And then to find out he was staying there—

"Ronan?" Even her voice fills him with longing. "Ronan, look at me."

He looks. Her face is deadly serious. There are little lines shooting straight up from the bridge of her nose. Her lips are pressed together tightly. He can't tell what she's thinking. He's never been able to tell. When his mother told him that Jordie had been at the house, he felt as if his heart had stopped in his chest. Jordie? At the house? What did she want?

"She wants you to call her," his mother had said. But boy, he had to think about that. *Why* did she want to talk to him? Was she angry with him? Did she hate him? Did she think he killed Maugham? She saw the police take him away in handcuffs.

Now he finds out that she lied to the police—for him. She didn't tell them the real reason he went to her house. But the way she's looking at him now, he simply can't fathom why she lied.

"Ronan, I know Derek went home that night to get the bracelet. But the police didn't find it on him."

"The police know about the bracelet?" He can't stop himself from asking. Nor can he stop the hammering of his heart in his chest.

She shakes her head. "No one knows about it—except you and I. *I* know Derek went home. I also know what the police found on him—there wasn't any bracelet. And it's not in his room. I know because I looked."

She's staring hard at him. It reminds him of how the cops look at him, that unwavering, unflinching latching of their eyes on his, trying to fake him out, trying to make him believe they already know everything there is to know about him because what's in his head is leaking out through his eyes.

"Ronan, your mother was wearing it when I went to talk to her."

He doesn't know what to say.

"You have to tell me what happened, Ronan. You have to tell me because it's scaring me to think about it."

How can he speak? He can barely breathe. If she's put together the pieces she has, and if she's come to believe he really did it, that he really killed Maugham, then there's no way she's going to keep everything to herself forever. She's not that kind of person. She would never protect someone she knows to be a murderer.

"Ronan, you have to talk to me. You have to tell me. Derek went home to get that bracelet, but he never came back. They found one of your buttons right beside his body. Your mother is wearing the bracelet. She told me when you gave it to her."

He feels like a drowning man, swirling around and around, unable to draw a single breath, unable to do anything but thrash about helplessly.

"Did you follow Derek from my house?"

"Follow him? No. No."

Jordie nods, but the gesture is so slight, he almost misses it. "Because you couldn't have known he was going to go home that night," she says. "I didn't even know." Her eyes never waver from his. "But you saw him. You talked to him, didn't you?"

The word comes out before he can stop it. "Yes."

"Tell me."

"I ran into him on the trail behind his house."

He watches as her shoulders slump. She's like a balloon with a leak. She deflates in slow motion.

"What were you doing there?"

"I didn't kill him, Jordie." He can't let her believe for even a second that he did.

"Then how did your button end up where it did?"

She's a hound after a fox; she's not going to let up. He can log off his computer. He can refuse to talk to her. But that will just make it worse—and nothing, he knows, will make it better.

"We had an argument," he says finally.

"Argument? And?" When he can't think what to say next, she adds, "Did your button jump off your jacket? Is that what happened?"

Jesus, such a beautiful girl, and such cutting sarcasm, like a butcher knife slicing into his heart.

"It got physical," he admits. If she tells the police that, he's screwed for sure.

"How physical?"

"I didn't want to talk to him at all, Jordie. I didn't even see him until it was too late. It was snowing, you remember? And it was blowing. I was walking with my head down, and all of a sudden, there he was in front of me. He was pissed off right away."

"Why? Why was he pissed off?"

Ronan feels heat in his cheeks. He's sure he looks like a kid caught red-handed stealing cake from the kitchen—or like a killer standing over the body with a smoking gun.

"I guess he didn't expect to see me there, and when he did, he was naturally suspicious."

"Naturally?"

"Because there's not much up there except his house," Ronan says, which, he knows, raises the question, So what were you doing there? Sure enough:

"So what were you doing there, Ronan?"

If he tells her, how does he know she won't go and tell the cops? But if he doesn't tell her, well, how does he know she won't tell the cops the parts that so far she hasn't told them?

"Ronan?"

He looks into the screen, into her eyes, and he starts to talk. He talks slowly, watching her the whole time. He sees worry in her eyes. He sees surprise. He sees shock. And then more worry. Deep worry. So deep that it scares him.

"Did anyone see you, Ronan?" she asks when he's finally said all there is to say.

"There was no one down there, Jordie. I told you that. Just him."

"What about before that?"

"Before?"

"Before you ran into Derek. Did anyone see you?"

He thinks about that night. He walked from his house to Jordie's house through streets that were completely deserted. It was cold and snowing. It was after Christmas, when everyone was partied out and stuffed full of turkey and cranberry sauce, shortbread and chocolate, eggnog, spiked and plain—all the treats that make an appearance once a year. Everyone was inside, warm and dozing if they were adults, playing with toys if they were little kids, hanging out with friends or relatives if they were older. He remembers perfectly how it felt—like walking through a ghost town or, even, like being a ghost walking unseen through a town filled with pleased and satisfied citizens. He had felt so alone as he made that walk. His hand had actually trembled as he reached out to ring her doorbell. And then later, when he walked away, it was more of the same, more being alone in a town full of people, none of whom meant anything to him...well, except for the person he was leaving. The person who was tucked up in her house with that jerk Maugham, and it was his own fault because he'd been idiot enough to let her go—hell, to push her away. You are the author of your own misfortune, Ronan, no doubt about that. He doesn't plan to tell her, but the truth is that he felt sorry for himself as he disappeared again into the gathering snow.

"Jesus, Ronan."

She's annoyed now, the way she was at the end, before he told her maybe it was better for them not to be together anymore.

"Why do you always have to do this? Why do you make me do all the work?" she says.

"Sorry." It's the first time he's said that to her, and she knows it. Her eyes widen. She looks slightly stunned, as if he were speaking to her now in Latin or ancient Greek. "I just—" he begins. Just what? Just answer the question. *Did anyone see you, Ronan?* "No, I don't think so."

"You don't *think* so?"

"No."

"Are you sure? Did you think maybe you saw someone but you're not sure—is that it? If you saw someone, then maybe that person saw you."

"What difference does it make?" He's up to his neck in it, and everything he's just told Jordie makes it worse for him. "If someone saw me before or after I ran into Derek, but they didn't see Derek after I left, when, I swear, he was still alive, what difference does it make?"

"You're in big trouble, Ronan. The cops think you killed him."

The cops think.

He catches his breath. To ask or not to ask, that is the question.

"What about you? What do you think?" It's what he's wanted to know all along. It's the only thing he's wanted to know.

"If you want to convince the cops, Ronan, you have to think. You have to have a solid story."

What is she saying—that she believes him? That she wants to believe him but it's up to him to convince her? That she doesn't care whether he did it or not but that if he wants to stay free, he'd better find a way to convince the cops?

"I didn't see anyone," he says. But is that right?

"What?" she says. She's leaning into the computer, searching his face. "There's something. I can see it in your eyes. What is it?"

He's shaking his head even as he starts to tell her. "It was a domestic."

"A domestic? You mean a housekeeper or a nanny, like that?"

"A domestic dispute. But they were too wrapped up in themselves to notice me. I'd stake my life on it."

"You *are* staking your life on it, Ronan." She's got those two lines over the bridge of her nose again. "Tell me about it anyway. Where were you? What did you see?"

"Trust me, Jordie, when people are in the middle of something like that—"

"Humor me, Ronan."

He begins to talk again.

An hour later, Jordie is staring at a blank computer screen and wondering. Ronan is telling the truth about some things—she's sure of it. Either that or he's a complete idiot because, really, how hard will it be to check on what he's told her? Also, he has absolutely no guarantee that some of what he's said will even help him. But he's put it out there, and that part is checkable too. The question is, so what? What does it all mean? Do the things that are checkable prove anything? Do they even come close to proving that the cops are wrong about Ronan?

She thinks about this all night. When you come right down to it, what has she found out? What use is it? What can she do with it? What *should* she do with it?

Twenty-One

Jordie is antsy the whole of the next day. She can't remember the last time she's had so much trouble concentrating. All she can think about is what Ronan has told her and what kept her awake all night.

The morning passes. She meets up with some girlfriends for lunch but finds herself uninterested in what they're saying—one is planning a trip to the city to spend the Christmas money she got from her grandparents, one met a guy while visiting relatives three hundred miles away and is now fretting about the difficulties of long-distance relationships, and a third bemoans the fact that she has neither money nor a boyfriend and then starts apologizing to Jordie as soon as she voices the thought: "I'm not being insensitive, honest."

Jordie rewraps her tuna sandwich and stands up. "It's okay," she tells the girl. She walks away without another word. Behind her, one of her friends says to the girl, "See what you've done? Jesus, Derek *died!*"

In the schoolyard, Jordie takes out her phone and makes a call. She gets the same answer she got earlier in the morning, which is to say no answer at all. When the bell rings, she heads to English class. Ms. Phillips has just started Act I, Scene I of *Hamlet* when an announcement comes over the PA system. Jordie is called to the office.

She sees Sergeant Tritt through the glass wall. He is standing facing her and comes to open the door for her.

"Your principal has put an office at our disposal," Tritt says. "Third on the right."

It's Ms. Syros's office. They go inside and Tritt closes the door. He waves her into a chair and then grabs the chair from behind the desk and places it so that he can sit facing her.

"What did you want to talk to me about, Jordie?" he asks.

"It's about what happened to Derek."

Tritt sits at attention, leaning forward so that he is on the very edge of invading her space. He waits.

"I talked to Ronan," she says.

"Okay."

"He says he ran into Derek that night."

"Ran into him?"

"Behind Derek's house. Right near where they found Derek."

If Tritt were an insect, his antennae would be all aquiver, Jordie thinks.

"He says he had an argument with Derek."

"An argument?"

"And that it got kind of physical."

"I see."

"He says Derek grabbed him and that's how that button ended up where it did."

"The button from Ronan's jacket, you mean."

Jordie nods. She hopes she is doing the right thing, but she can't think of anything else to do.

"They kind of got physical and Derek grabbed Ronan and pulled the button off."

"Did Ronan say what he was doing over there behind Derek's house?" Tritt asks.

"Yes." Ronan was so honest with her that it alarmed her. She tells Tritt about the bracelet.

"This whole thing is about a bracelet?" Tritt is shaking his head, as if she's told him that Derek got killed over something as trivial as a pack of cigarettes or a twenty-dollar bill.

"That's how it started," Jordie says.

Tritt leans back in his chair now. "That boy must have it bad for you, young lady."

"What do you mean?"

"Confessing to murder? Giving you all the details? It's clear he wants you to forgive him." He pauses. "You tell them, 'You'll feel better when you get it off your chest.' Half the time—more than half the time—they don't listen. But with this kid?" He shakes his head again.

"He didn't confess to murder," Jordie says quietly.

"Well, okay, so technically he didn't. But you're a smart girl. You do realize that everything you've told me just seals the deal, don't you? He's just put himself at the scene of the crime. We have physical evidence of that, but now we have him telling someone he was there. We have him getting into an altercation with the victim." He glances at her. "Sorry. With Derek. And we have the motive—the bracelet. You knew where you were going with this when you asked to see me, didn't you, Jordie?"

Jordie sits tall and straight. "He says he didn't kill Derek, and I believe him. He says he ran into Derek and that they had an argument. But he swears Derek was fine when he left him."

Tritt leans forward again. "He left him in the exact location where he was found, with a button from his jacket beside the bod—beside Derek. But you're telling me that you believe him when he says Derek was still standing?"

"Yes." She says it firmly and without even a second's hesitation.

Tritt lets out a long sigh. "But you do realize that what you've told me makes things even worse for Ronan, right?"

"That isn't why I called you," Jordie says. "There's more."

"Now you're going to tell me that not only did Ronan *not* kill Derek, but that he knows who did. Maybe he passed a stranger on his way back to wherever he was going. Or maybe—"

"I don't think he knows who did it," Jordie says.

Tritt studies her. "But?"

"But I think I do."

It's Saturday, and Renee, the home-care nurse, isn't there all day the way she is during the week. She'll drop by around noon and help Ronan's mother with her personal care. She'll check her vitals too. So Ronan makes a soft-boiled egg for his mother and manages to get her to eat most of it. He gets some tea into her, too, but she drinks it clear, so there are no calories there, no nutrition.

"You should have some milk," Ronan says. "Or some juice."

His mother shakes her head. "I can't."

Ronan debates with himself: make her drink some milk, or let her be? She's wasting away day by day. She was never what you might call hefty, but now she is like a tissue-wrapped skeleton. Her skin is almost translucent, and her bones stand out in relief. Her eyes are sunken and no longer sparkle like they used to when she laughs. But then, she no longer laughs. Even smiling seems to take more effort than she can manage. It won't be long. He knows it, and she knows it. He tries not to think about it, at least not while he is in her presence. If he thinks about it, he chokes up. Sometimes he cries. Jeez, if the kids at school saw that, they'd never steer clear of him again. Or maybe they would. Nothing makes people more uncomfortable than a guy who cries in public. Better to put your fist through a wall. Or through some other kid. And better by far to do almost anything at all than to let his mother see him burst into tears. She's doing her best to be strong, and she's told him that she's counting on him to do the same. "We have to be strong together" is how she puts it. She also reassures him—which he hates—that there is money set aside for his education. She wants him to go to university. She wants him to make something of himself. She wishes she could do more for him, but she can't, and she's sorry about that.

He decides to let her be. A glass of milk isn't worth an argument. It isn't worth draining her strength.

"You should take a nap, Mom," he says. "I'm going to go clean up the kitchen."

She reaches out and squeezes his hand. "You're a good boy. I love you, Ronan."

"I love you too, Mom." He bends down and kisses her on the forehead. Her skin is cool and dry, like paper. He takes the tray with the egg cup on it and the mug still half filled with tea.

He cleans up, just as he said he would. He sets her dishes into the dishwasher along with his cereal bowl and the plate he used for his toast. He wipes the toast crumbs off the counter and puts the jam back in the fridge. Then he sits down to wait.

Half an hour later, he tiptoes upstairs and checks on his mother. She is sound asleep, and if the past few weeks are anything to go on, she will sleep for hours. He leaves a note on her bedside table, where she is sure to see it. He goes back downstairs, puts on sneakers—his boots won't fit over the device that's attached to his ankle—and pulls on his coat. He grabs his hat, gloves and keys. He locks the front door behind him and starts down the front walk.

The ankle device starts beeping before he hits the sidewalk, but that doesn't stop him. He keeps walking. He's still walking when a patrol car pulls up in front of him and two cops get out, one near the front of the car, the second back a ways, both ready to unholster their weapons. Ronan puts his hands up. He tells them, yes, he knows he's violated his bail conditions, and yes, he knows what that means. He offers no resistance when they handcuff him and pat him down. When one of them puts his hand on Ronan's head to guide him into the squad car's backseat, Ronan informs them that he wants to talk to Lieutenant Diehl. One of the cops laughs.

"Don't worry," he says. "He's waiting for you back at the station house."

At the police station, Ronan is rebooked and led into another room. He's only there for a few minutes before he is taken into an interview room. This time, because he is under arrest and in violation of his bail conditions, he is handcuffed to an iron loop set into the heavy table. He is left there, and it seems as if an eternity passes. He starts to worry about his mother waking up in an empty house to a note that is sure to raise more questions—and worry—than it answers. He begins to imagine her becoming frantic and wonders how that will affect her. What if she tries to get up on her own before Renee arrives? What if she falls down the stairs? What if, in doing all of that, she takes the oxygen tube off, or it comes off? He stands up abruptly and is jerked back by the hand-cuff. This is all a mistake. He shouldn't have walked out of the house like that. He should never have come here.

The door opens and Diehl steps into the room, a cup of coffee in one hand, a donut in the other. He grins at Ronan.

"Going somewhere, sport?" he says.

Ronan sits down again. What else can he do?

Diehl comes another pace into the room so that the door can close behind him. He pops the rest of the donut into his mouth and washes it down with a gulp of coffee.

"So," he says, "I hear you want to see me."

Ronan settles himself. He pushes all thoughts of his mother from his head and instead fixes his attention on Diehl. "That's right," he says.

Diehl polishes off the rest of his coffee and tosses the paper cup into a garbage can in the corner of the room. He grabs the chair opposite Ronan and drops down onto it.

"I'm all ears," he says.

Ronan looks around. There's a mirror on one wall. Ronan isn't fooled by it any more than anyone else who gets put in this room. He knows that whoever is on the other side can see into the room even if he can't see them. He also knows that they can hear him, so he leans across the table to Diehl and whispers, "What I have to say you probably don't want anyone else to hear." In case Diehl doesn't get it, he nods at the mirror.

Diehl's eyes are impossible to read. He looks right at Ronan, but Ronan can't get a fix on what he's thinking.

"Is that right?" Diehl says in a normal voice. "And why is that?"

"Trust me," Ronan says.

Diehl laughs heartily, as if this is the funniest thing he has heard in a long time.

"Trust you? Why would I do that, Ronan?"

Ronan leans even farther across the table, as far as the handcuff will allow him. His whisper is even softer: "Because it wasn't Derek. It was me."

Diehl's face hardens. For a moment, Ronan thinks he is going to say something. Or maybe he's going to do something. Something that Ronan won't like and won't be able to defend himself against.

But he doesn't.

He looks at Ronan as if he's studying a new specimen of vermin. Then he stands up, crosses to the mirror and pulls down a blind, making the mirror disappear. He also flicks a switch on the wall. He sits down again, his face harder than ever.

"Suppose you tell me what you're talking about," he says.

Ronan notes that big, bad, supercool and unflappable Lieutenant Diehl has impatience in his eyes.

"It wasn't Derek you saw that night. It was me."

Diehl shakes his head. "I don't know what you're talking about."

But there's a wariness to Diehl now. It's in the way he watches Ronan, in the quick lick of his lips, in the glance at the blinds covering the mirror, as if to make sure.

"Sure you do." Ronan settles in. "You know, and I know. And I want a deal."

"A deal?" Diehl forces a laugh. "For what?"

"You don't go to prison, and neither do I."

"Me go to prison? For what?"

"For what you did to your wife."

Aha! It flits through his eyes like a bird on the wing— it's there, it's gone. But Ronan recognizes panic when he sees it.

"And what is it you think I did to my wife?" Diehl relaxes back in his chair, his posture a mirror of Ronan's.

"You forced her out of the house."

"Right," Diehl says. "Now that we have the goods on you, you just happen to remember something you never brought up before. Or should I say you spin me one? Nice try, kid." He starts to get up.

"I didn't know before that you live across the street from Maugham." Ronan says the words calmly, like it's no skin off his nose if Diehl walks out on him. He can tell his story to any cop in the building. "I didn't find out until yesterday. Your wife was that teacher, the one that had to retire when she got Alzheimer's, the one that supposedly walked away from your house when you were asleep. Only you weren't asleep that night. And she didn't just walk away. You forced her out. I saw you. It wasn't Derek. It was me."

Diehl is standing behind the chair. His eyes are narrowed.

"That's some story," he says.

"It's a true story."

"But who's going to believe it?"

"Everyone. Because I can prove it."

Diehl laughs. "Is that right?" The cocky bastard.

"Yes, it is. For starters, I can prove where I was that night. I was in the Maughams' house. I broke in. I can prove that too. I can also prove exactly when I was there."

"So now you're not just a murderer. You're a burglar too. Suppose you tell me all about that."

Ronan shakes his head. "You drop the charges against me. You let me go. You say you made a mistake. I walk away, and I don't tell anyone what you did to your wife— and what you did to Derek."

"Oh? So now I did something to the Maugham kid too?"

Ronan has to hand it to Diehl. Maybe he was nervous at first, but he sure isn't now. Is there something Ronan has overlooked? He glances around the room. They're in here alone. Diehl could do anything to him and no one would be the wiser until it was too late, and Ronan is confident that Diehl could spin his own story about why the kid who was arrested for murder is lying dead on the floor, maybe shot with Diehl's gun.

"You killed him because you thought he saw what you did."

"Uh-huh." Diehl is all boredom. "And I suppose you can prove that too."

He wants to know what I have, Ronan thinks. He wants everything so he can get rid of me and explain everything away.

"You came over to the house," Ronan says. "You rang the bell."

If Ronan had so much as blinked an eye, he would have missed it. But he didn't blink, and there it is: Diehl flinching.

"I heard you. You rang the bell. And when no one answered and you didn't see anyone leaving the house, you went around behind the house to see if Derek had gone that way, along the trail. You saw us, didn't you?"

"Us?"

"Me and Derek. You saw us. We were having an argument. It got kind of physical."

"So now you're admitting you were physical with the Maugham kid." Diehl seems genuinely amused. "That's it, kid. Come clean. It'll do you good."

"You killed Derek. And you've been trying to pin it on me ever since."

"It's a nice story," Diehl says. "But that's all it is. A story."

"I know why you did it."

Diehl's face hardens.

"I know the blood is still there."

"What blood?" Diehl tries to convey by how he asks the question that he doesn't believe that for a second.

"When you wouldn't let her in, she hammered on the door. She hammered on it until her knuckles bled. I know that because when I found out who she was, I went back through the papers. They said she was found with bloody knuckles. They guessed she'd tried to find shelter but couldn't get in. They were right. Only that shelter was her own house—the one you locked her out of."

"I've had enough of these fairy tales," Diehl says. "You breached the terms of your bail. You're going back to lockup."

"I know you think you got rid of it," Ronan says. "But you didn't. Not all of it. And from what I've heard, they don't need much blood to make a match."

Just like that, Diehl's face is inches from Ronan's. "You're threatening the wrong guy, you little creep. There is no blood on that door."

"You're sure of that?" Ronan smiles, refusing to let Diehl see how he really feels.

"Yeah, I'm sure."

"What about in your truck?" Ronan knows he's scored a direct hit when he sees the look on Diehl's face. "I saw you put her in the truck—before you came across the street and rang the bell. She didn't walk away, did she? You drove her away. You wanted to make sure she didn't come back."

"I'm going to bury you, kid," Diehl says. "Just like that." He snaps his fingers. "You have a record. It'd be just like a kid with your past to start spinning stories. They sound kind of desperate, if you want my opinion. You need to face reality. You need to take responsibility. We've got a motive for you, and from what you've just told me, you were at the scene and you admit being physical with the Maugham kid. And once your mother kicks it, there's not a soul left in this world who will give a good goddamn about you. So if you think you can threaten me—"

Diehl is a big man. A big man with a gun and a badge. Ronan has to swallow hard to rid himself of the fear that comes at him.

"Fine," he says. "I want to see my lawyer. And when he gets here, I'm going to tell him everything I know. Then we'll see who believes what. Especially when you come into all that money. Jesus, talk about motive." Diehl isn't happy about that—Ronan can see it in his eyes.

"A couple million dollars, isn't that right? That's what the old man got for his farm when he sold it to that developer. And he earmarked every single dime of it for your wife's care." Jordie told him that. She says it's common knowledge. "The only way you could touch it is if she died. Kind of convenient the way things worked out, huh?" He forces a confidence he doesn't feel.

"I've had just about enough of you, kid," Diehl says. He pulls out a key and approaches the table to uncuff Ronan.

Behind him, the door to the interview room opens, and Sergeant Tritt walks in.

"What's up, Mike?" he asks.

"The kid walked out of his mother's house," Diehl says. "He's going back to lockup. Handle it for me, will you, Neil? I have something to take care of." He tosses the key to Tritt and leaves the room.

"Come on, kid," Tritt says.

Twenty-Two

With Ronan Barthe safely behind bars again, Neil Tritt stops to talk to a couple of patrol officers and then gets into his car and heads north. He parks a couple hundred yards from his destination, below the crest of the hill, retrieves some equipment from the trunk of his car and trudges up the steep slope. He stops near the top, where he can see without attracting attention to himself. His heart sinks when he sees what's happening. He raises the camera that he has taken from the car, adjusts the telephoto lens and starts snapping pictures. When he's done, he trudges back to his car and stows the camera. Then it's back up the hill again.

He's halfway up the driveway before the person he's come to see even notices him. Mike Diehl is standing outside his front door. There's a bucket of steaming water on the top step, and Diehl is holding a wet rag in his gloved hands. The garage door stands open. Diehl straightens when he realizes he isn't alone anymore. He grins at Tritt.

"Just getting that frost off so I can see if it builds up again—you know, to see if I really am leaking heat like you say," Diehl says.

"Good idea," Tritt says. He continues up the driveway until he is standing beside Diehl. He sniffs the air, and his heart sinks lower. "Washing it at the same time, I see," he says.

"Huh?"

"The bleach. I can smell it."

"Oh," Diehl says. "Yeah. So, the kid's going back to detention, huh?"

"Looks that way," Tritt says. "For now anyway."

"For now? Come on, Neil, you don't think the judge is going to spring him on compassionate grounds again, do you?"

"Maybe," Tritt says. "Under the circumstances."

Diehl snorts. "Any judge that'd do that should step down from the bench—on mental-deficiency grounds." He drops the rag into the bucket and bends to pick it up.

"Let me get that," Tritt says. He slips in smoothly, grabs the bucket by the handle and starts for the garage. Diehl trots after him. Inside the garage, the back door to the truck stands open. Tritt can see a layer of frost on the backseat. He sets the bucket down, sticks his head inside the back of the truck and sniffs the seat. He shakes his head. "She was a nice woman, Mike. And I mean that. A nice woman and a real lady."

"I miss her, that's for sure," Diehl says. "I missed her for months before she walked off the way she did. It's a terrible disease, Neil. It takes the person and leaves the shell. She didn't know who she was or what she was doing. Everything confused her."

"You mean *almost* everything, don't you, Mike?"

Diehl frowns.

"She knew enough to want to get in out of the cold, isn't that right?" Tritt says.

"You mean the blood on her knuckles?" It seems to Tritt that Diehl is working hard to keep his tone neutral.

"And the blood on your front door," Tritt says. "And on this seat here."

"What are you talking about?" Diehl asks, still working it hard, seeming puzzled now, as if he's wondering what his old friend and colleague is blathering about.

"That switch, the one in the interview room. I disengaged it, Mike. You thought you turned off the audio, but you didn't."

Diehl still doesn't give up. "That kid is all bluster. He said he wanted to make a deal and wanted me to throw the switch. But he's full of it. All that talk about blood on my door? Come on, Neil."

Tritt looks his old friend in the eye. "Right," he says. "Because if there was any blood—and whatever there was would have been pretty microscopic after you washed the door the morning after Elise disappeared—it's gone now, is that it? Same for anything that might have been in this truck. Right again?"

Diehl says nothing.

Tritt reaches for his phone and flips it open. He says one word: "Now." Then he looks back at Diehl. "I talked to the kid yesterday. I had forensics out here this morning while you were talking to him. Had them give your truck a once-over. What they found backs the kid up, Mike. She didn't walk away. She was driven away."

"If you're going to believe that, I want a lawyer," Diehl says.

A patrol car slides up Diehl's driveway. As the two uniformed officers get out, Tritt says, "You couldn't wait? What she had—that's a death sentence. You couldn't do right by her and make do with whatever was left over?"

"I want a lawyer," Diehl says again.

Tritt nods at the two officers, who circle Diehl and start to cuff him. Diehl offers no resistance as Tritt places a hand on his shoulder and tells him he is under arrest.

Jordie Cross is seated in the foyer of the police station. It's nearly five o'clock. She should call her mother and tell her she will be late for supper so her mother doesn't worry. But if she makes the call, she will have to lie to her mother about where she is, and she doesn't want to lie anymore, not to anyone. She waits. Maybe Sergeant Tritt will appear soon. Maybe whatever he wants to talk to her about won't take long and she can get home for supper after all. Besides, she wants to know what happened. She doesn't want to make do with an abbreviated version on the news. So she waits, leaving her cell phone in her pocket, where it has been for the past hour.

It's ten minutes before Tritt appears through a door to the right of the desk sergeant. He beckons to her, holding the door, and leads her to a kitchen-like room—the break room, he calls it—and invites her to sit. He offers coffee. She declines.

"Do you mind if I have one?" he asks. "It's been a long day."

Of course she doesn't mind. But that doesn't stop her right foot from thrumming impatiently as she watches him pour coffee from a carafe, stir in sugar, add milk, stir that in and then carry the mug over to the table, where he sits, sighs and takes a sip.

"Did you find it?" Jordie asks. "Did you find blood where Ronan said you would?"

"We did," Tritt says. "On the front door and inside the truck. We got to the traces before Diehl. There's no way to prove how long it was there, but given that Diehl chose to clean it up after he talked to Ronan, well, that gives credence to Ronan's interpretation of events. Diehl is under arrest."

"Okay," Jordie says slowly. She's puzzled by Tritt's choice of words—*Ronan's interpretation of events.*

"What about Derek's clock? Was it still there or had Mrs. Maugham thrown it out?"

"It was there. And then there's the window, the one he said. The Maughams probably wouldn't have noticed it had been jimmied until spring, when they opened it. So that's another factor that backs up Ronan as a witness to what he says he saw."

There it is again—what he *says* he saw.

"As for the clock—Mrs. Maugham is positive the clock was undamaged when she and her husband left town. Ronan claims it broke at midnight the night he was in the house. The time and date displayed on the clock back that up. So unless Derek was in his room that night and broke the clock at that precise time, and unless Ronan broke in some time after that—"

"Wait a minute," Jordie says. "Are you saying you don't believe Ronan?"

Tritt takes another sip of his coffee. "I believe, based on the evidence, that Mike Diehl facilitated his wife's death. I believe that in doing what he did that night, he knew that she would die. He's been charged with first-degree murder. Whether that charge sticks or gets argued down to second-degree or manslaughter, I don't know. His lawyer will probably try to argue mercy killing. But given the amount of money Diehl stands to inherit pursuant to Elise's death, that could be difficult.

The fact that we have all this is thanks to you and Ronan. But—"

Here it comes, thinks Jordie.

"Jordie, I want you to tell me everything you know about the night Derek died."

"I already did." Why is he even asking? He doesn't think she had something to do with it, does he?

Tritt leans forward, his hands clasped in front of him on the table.

"I also want you to tell me about any conversation you might have had with Ronan before Derek disappeared, before his body was found, before Ronan was arrested and before this morning. And I want you to tell me the absolute truth, without leaving anything out."

Jordie is stunned by this request. But she also feels the blood rising in her face. He is telling her he knows—not suspects, but knows—that she has held back certain things in past conversations. And he's right about that. He's telling her he knows she has spoken to Ronan, several times, about what happened, and that she hasn't mentioned most of that either. But is he also telling her that he doesn't trust her?

"Why?" she asks.

"Because I need to know."

They look at each other, the cop and the girl. Jordie tries to read Tritt the way she suspects he can read her. But all she sees is a man who wants to know more than he thinks he does already. So she begins to tell him. She has no idea how long she talks. Tritt listens without moving. He doesn't write anything down. He doesn't ask any questions, not until she finally stops talking.

"And that's it?" he says. "That's everything—every conversation you had with Ronan, everything he said to you and everything you said to him?"

"Everything that I can remember," she says. "Why? He was right about Lieutenant Diehl, wasn't he? You believe what he said he saw, don't you?"

"That's not the problem," Tritt says.

"Then what is?"

"Jordie, did it ever occur to you that Ronan might have killed Derek? Maybe Derek attacked him, or maybe they got into a fight and it got out of hand, but that he did do it?"

"No, of course not!" Jordie is indignant. But as soon as she says the words, she realizes what she's doing. "Well, maybe when I saw the police officer with that button, I might have thought that."

"The button." Tritt nods. He unclasps his hands and reaches for his coffee. He takes a sip. "Let's say Ronan was in Derek's house and saw what he saw. There's no reason to think he wasn't. But let's say it plays out this way: Ronan saw Diehl, but Diehl didn't see him. It's possible. Diehl hasn't said anything about seeing anyone that night—not when he was talking to Ronan this morning, not when he was talking to me just recently, not anytime. In fact, he denies that he saw anyone."

"If he didn't see anyone—if he didn't see *someone* and assume it was Derek—then why would he kill Derek?" Jordie says.

"That *is* the question."

They look at each other again.

"We have nothing to tie Diehl to Derek's murder," Tritt says after a moment. "No physical evidence at all. We'll keep looking. There's a forensic team at his house even as we speak. But—"

"But he's a cop," Jordie says. "A detective. He knows what you'd look for. He washed off the blood. Maybe he wasn't thorough, but he knew no one would doubt his story. It's only because Ronan saw him—" She stops, thinking about the implication of what she has just said.

"Diehl denies that he saw anyone," Tritt says again. "It's possible he's lying. But it's also possible he's telling the truth."

"But if he didn't do it—"

"Ronan admits he saw Derek that night. He admits being in a physical altercation with him. And we have physical evidence of that."

"The button," Jordie says.

Tritt nods. "So with regard to Derek, we really have two possible suspects. And each one is pointing at the other. Each one claims that the other had a motive for killing Derek. I'm not sure if the charges against Ronan will be dropped or not. It depends on the Crown, on which one they think they can make a case against. But let's say, for sake of argument, that they retain the charge against Ronan. Well, I don't think his lawyer will have much trouble sowing reasonable doubt in the minds of the jury, and that's assuming it ever gets past a preliminary inquiry."

Jordie has to think about this for a moment. While she thinks, Tritt makes it crystal clear.

"The way I see it unfolding, if Diehl gets charged, his lawyer is going to paint Ronan as Derek's murderer. If Ronan gets charged, his lawyer has plenty to go on to hang it on Diehl. Either way, there's going to be enough reasonable doubt to flummox a jury. It's even possible that if one gets off, the other will get charged—and get off. On the other hand, they could convict. You never know with a jury."

"You mean Ronan could be charged with murdering Derek—and found guilty?" Jordie says. Ever since Ronan told her about that night, she has never considered that possibility.

"You could put it that way," Tritt says.

"So he's still under arrest?"

"He's being held until the Crown sorts out the charges."

Twenty-Three

In April, three months after Diehl is arrested and charged with the murder of his wife and of Derek Maugham, Diane Barthe dies. Jordie hears about it from her mother, who heard it from a friend of hers who worked for the home-care agency that had been providing care to Mrs. Barthe and who knew that Jordie had been seeing Ronan at one time. There is no notice in the newspaper, and Jordie has to visit every funeral home in town before she finds the one that received the body. She is told that there was no service.

"Why not?"

"The deceased was cremated."

"Already? But she only just died."

"The deceased has been cremated," the funeral director, a middle-aged man with a soft voice, says again. "I am afraid that is all I can tell you."

If Jordie wants to know any more, she will have to talk to Ronan.

He's stopped coming to school. Jordie thinks she can guess why. He never made many friends, and there are still a lot of kids—a lot of other people too—who are convinced that he killed Derek and got away with it. He's called and texted Jordie's cell dozens of times, but so far she hasn't answered. Every time she thinks about Ronan, she thinks about that button. Maybe Diehl really did do it. Maybe he deserved to get charged. Maybe Tritt came up with more evidence against him, and maybe that will come out at the trial. But—and there is something in her that's ashamed to admit it—maybe Ronan really did get away with something. Maybe he did exactly what she worried he'd done when she first realized that button was his. Maybe he did what she thought Diehl had done after she realized what Ronan had seen that night. Maybe he took the opportunity to point the finger at Diehl.

But now his mother has died. There are certain things you have to do in life whether you want to or not. You have to go to school. You have to brush your teeth and clean your room, and when you are old enough, you have to do your own laundry.

You also have to acknowledge the passing of people you know or whose families you know. You have to show that you care. You have to pay your respects. These things, she knows, even if others don't, are not optional.

There is a For Sale sign in front of Ronan's house. Slapped across it is a second, smaller sign: Sold. Both signs hit her with the force of blows to the belly. She hasn't seen Ronan or spoken to him in months, but somehow it has never occurred to her that he is going to leave.

She walks past the signs and climbs the steps to the porch. She rings the doorbell. She can hear it sound inside the house. It seems louder than she remembers and echoes in what she now imagines is an empty house.

She waits. No one answers.

She rings again.

When there is still no answer, she steps to the living room window and tries to look inside. But the curtains, made of heavy fabric, are drawn. She can see nothing on the other side of them.

She goes back down the steps and stands in the driveway, looking up at the house. He can't have gone already. But there is nothing to hold him here. His mother is dead. His father is long gone. The cremation has already happened. The house is sold.

She has no idea where he might have gone. She could ask the real estate agent whose name and photograph are on the For Sale sign. But she knows Ronan well enough to guess that he has volunteered no information. If he is gone, he is gone, and that's that.

She digs in her purse for a notebook and pen. She scrawls a note—*If you get this, call me*—signs her name and goes back to the porch to shove the note through the letter slot in the front door. She hears it hit the floor with a soft little scrabble. She hears nothing else.

As she starts down the street, she casts one last glance over her shoulder. A curtain flutters in the front bedroom window. It's probably just a draft, she thinks. It's an old house.

Norah McClintock writes mystery and crime fiction for young adult readers. She is the author of the Chloe and Levesque, Mike and Riel, Robyn Hunter, and Ryan Dooley series, as well as many stand-alone novels. Norah grew up in Montreal, Quebec, is a graduate of McGill University (in history, of all things) and lives in Toronto, Ontario. She is a five-time winner of the Crime Writers of Canada's Arthur Ellis Award for Best Juvenile Crime Novel. Her novels have been translated into sixteen languages. Visit www.norahmcclintock.com for more information.